# RANSOMED DAUGHTER

# ALSO BY ERIC P. BISHOP:

The Body Man

Breach of Trust (Coming in 2024)

The Omega Group (Coming in 2024)


For more info about Eric, please visit his website:

www.ericpbishop.com

or

You can contact him at eric@ericpbishop.com

# RANSOMED DAUGHTER

## A TROY EVANS NOVELLA

### ERIC P. BISHOP

BRUNOE MEDIA PUBLISHING

eBook ISBN-979-8-9888360-0-1

Paperback ISBN-979-8-9888360-1-8

Hardcover ISBN-979-8-9888360-2-5

Library of Congress Cataloging-in-Publication Identifiers: LCCN: 2023914745

Book Cover by J. Todd Wilkins Photography

First Edition October 2023

Printed in The United States of America

10 9 8 7 6 5 4 3 2 1

# PRAISE FOR THE BODY MAN & RANSOMED DAUGHTER

*"Thriller readers take note: there's a new sheriff in town."*
**--Ben Coes, New York Times Bestselling Author**

*"In a world of tired cliches, Eric has crafted the rip-roaring world of Troy Evans. This novella is a pure shot of intellectual adrenaline!"*
**--John Guarnieri, Security Director, Former USSS**

*"In a crowded field of today's political thrillers, The Body Man will keep you guessing until the final page."*
**--Don Bentley, NYT Bestselling Author of Tom Clancy's Target Acquired**

*"Action and intrigue abound in this fast-paced, one-two punch from the author who gave us The Body Man."*
**--A.M. Adair, Author of the Elle Anderson Series**

*"Heart pounding intensity, action filled, and heart-felt."*
**--Steve Stratton, Author of the Shadow Tier Series**

# DEDICATION

For Bruce & Noelle

Dream Big

Never Quit

Dad Loves You, Always

“Man is the cruelest animal.”

\- Nietzsche

# PART I - THE SNATCH

# 1

## VIENNA, AUSTRIA

A strong breeze passed through the square. The gust caused the leaves to swirl while the birds scurried under the tables in search of crumbs. The blast of air left those in its path refreshed on the abnormally warm spring day in Vienna.

Across from the café where Captain Troy Evans sat, St. Stephen's Cathedral glistened as rays of sunlight reflected off its imposing limestone walls. The towering Gothic structure with its multi-colored roof made for a magnificent backdrop. As he sat transfixed toward the structure, Troy's mind wandered. Architecture intrigued him, but after a few seconds, he glanced down at his watch. He only had a few minutes.

*Focus, dummy.* Troy reminded himself for the hundredth time.

With the late afternoon in full swing, the wide boulevard overflowed with scores of both locals and tourists alike. People passed by Troy's table as he glanced at them cautiously while doing his best to not make it obvious. Surveillance techniques were new to him, and Troy would be the first to admit he still had much to learn regarding the art of spycraft. The army transformed him into a good soldier, but did nothing to make him like Ethan Hunt.

Several women gave him more than a passing glance as they strolled by his table. Used to such things, Troy didn't give it a second thought. His rugged good looks and chiseled physique made him stand out from most average-looking men. He returned the friendly smiles, but was careful to look away quickly to discourage any of them from stopping. He had a job to do, and the colonel frowned upon his men attracting attention from strange foreign women, at least while they were on missions. Plus, it wasn't Troy's style.

His focus shifted. His eyes never stayed on the same object for more than a second or two. It had been a month since he and his team left the farm near Williamsburg, Virginia. While counterintelligence and spycraft skills require an immense amount of time to master, he and his team proved quick studies.

Today, instead of getting their feet wet, the colonel shoved them headfirst into a raging sea. Metaphorically speaking.

As he took in his surroundings, Troy observed a group of school-aged kids, no more than nine or ten years old, as they walked down the boulevard opposite the church square. Their laughter permeated the white noise around the basilica. Their ages made him think back to one of his many deployments, although the kids he encountered in Fallujah weren't as jovial and could not move around freely in public without fear of attack. These kids had no such encumbrances. Their banter made him recall his own childhood in Idaho. A carefree and happy time, Troy rarely thought of those days over the past several years. His life changed after the towers fell, and the scars of that fateful day still indirectly scarred his own flesh.

*O death, where is thy sting? O grave, where is thy victory?* The verse from his childhood came back as he reminisced about the past.

The children's laughter subsided a minute later as they took a side street from the boulevard. Troy glanced at his watch before his attention switched to a couple sitting on his right. They appeared to be in their late fifties. While the woman chain-smoked the moment she took her seat, the man opened a newspaper and ignored both her and his surroundings. A cloud of tobacco encompassed the woman on all sides as she breathed out a near-constant plume of acrid smoke. Troy hated cigarettes.

As he looked in the woman's direction, they made the briefest of eye contact. Decades older than him but still moderately attractive, the lavender dress clung to her body and made it clear she took care of herself. Most men would have taken a second look or even more. She pulled the cigarette out of her mouth long enough to smile before she took the next drag. The wide, toothy smile exposed her slightly crooked, moderately yellow-stained teeth. It negated any redeeming qualities she may have possessed, and he wondered why a woman who clearly valued her appearance would allow herself to have such wretched teeth. She exhaled another cloud of smoke in Troy's direction and said something.

Troy didn't understand any of the words directed at him. He shrugged and scrunched his face as he shook his head, hoping she would get the hint.

She didn't.

"I'm sorry, but I don't understand," Troy said in English as the woman continued to talk.

He was trying not to be rude but finally interrupted her when she didn't let up. "Look, ma'am, do you speak any English?"

The woman replied in words clearly not English.

"I take that as a no," Troy said tersely. His annoyance with the woman only grew.

She took several more drags and blew more puffs of smoke in his direction while she rambled her incoherent babble.

Troy's tone was anything but friendly as he spoke through gritted teeth, "If you don't put that damn thing out, I'm going to do it for you." The veins in his neck pulsed, and a large one in his temple bulged as he raised his voice. He had officially lost his cool.

"Calm down there, Cap." The voice emanated from the earbud hidden in his left ear.

Troy, his teammates called him Cap, turned away from the woman and slid his hand into his right front pocket. His fingers wrapped around the small cylinder-shaped device concealed out of sight as he keyed the button twice. In layman's terms, he acknowledged the comment with a *yes*. If he wanted to respond with a *no*, it would be a single tap.

"Yeah, you need to enhance your calm." A more sarcastic voice said over the comms.

Troy ignored the chatter and didn't key the mic. Although if he could have, he'd much preferred to thump the back of J.C. Kyle's head, the one who just told him to "enhance your calm." Everyone on the team not so lovingly referred to him as the Jackal. The nickname had nothing to do with the infamous terrorist known worldwide as Carlos the Jackal. In fact, the name stuck while in basic training nine years earlier since his first initial J, and last name Kyle sounded like the word Jackal. The name carried on throughout his military career.

Another voice interrupted the banter. "I've got eyes on the target, Cap. One hundred yards and closing." Perched high above them, Digger, real name Dave Riley, watched everything going on. Digger lay flat against the distant rooftop as his high-powered Leica binoculars watched the events unfold below.

At the sound of Digger's voice, Troy's focus returned to the task at hand. His annoyance at the cigarette lady bothered him enough to lose focus which wasn't a great way to start any mission.

*Focus, dammit. Get with the program, Troy.*

That little voice inside reminded him to compartmentalize and get better at letting things go. He wasn't used to being around civilians all that much. It had been years since he sat and relaxed at a café or restaurant. It felt foreign, and he was on edge to be around people without guns. No one was trying to kill him now, which should have provided him with some level of comfort, but ironically it had quite the opposite effect—it unnerved him.

Troy spent over a decade living in Iraq and Afghanistan inside Conex boxes or various other structures fighting the War on Terror. Often, he slept on the ground, his head propped up against his rucksack in an unforgiving environment. The military had limits on the lengths of soldiers' deployments, but Troy always found a loophole. With nothing for him back in the States, he was content to stay overseas as long as possible. Troy's newest role with The Omega Group afforded him opportunities that most in the military never experienced, but it took a toll on him, even though he would never admit it. There was nothing normal about his way of life.

With his newest assignment, Troy traded in his desert camo and rucksack for a collared shirt, pair of chinos, and worn loafers.

He felt naked.

Figuratively, if not literally.

The cool steel of the H&K, pressed against the small of his back, provided him limited comfort.

The Omega Group played by a unique set of rules, and it took some getting used to.

Troy knew the weapon was there, but only to be used if his life or the life of his men were in imminent danger. Vienna was not to turn into a shooting range. His mission parameters were extremely specific.

The colonel reminded him in no uncertain terms. *Vienna was not to turn into Baghdad, Mosul, or Kabul.*

"They just crossed from Stephansplatz onto Goldschmiedgasse. You should see them in ten seconds."

Digger's voice echoed in his ear. Troy keyed twice and looked toward the men who approached. His eyes settled on Terrance Wallace, who walked thirty feet in front of the target. The target followed the same path from the bank to his apartment each evening. Most people go with familiarity, but sometimes it leads to danger, especially if you're being hunted. The team had been in place for less than twenty-four hours, but because of the abundance of data available via geo-tracking, they could quickly piece together the target's movements on a day-by-day basis for the past several months.

Terrance, who everyone called Sarge, approached Troy's table at the outdoor café but never looked at his captain. The tall, muscular, dark-skinned man had a swagger about him. He was built like a tree trunk but moved with the speed of a short stop when everything went to pot. Nothing fazed Terrance, and he strolled past Troy seemingly without a care in the world.

Troy's eyes moved to his left and saw the man following behind Sarge. Troy gathered himself and slowly rose. He threw a twenty euro note on the table as he walked away and followed discretely behind the two men. He mirrored their path down Goldschmiedgasse and away from St. Stephen's.

As Troy quickened his pace, he looked down the wide stone boulevard and made eye contact with the Jackal, who leaned against a four-story building pretending to read the Oberösterreichische Nachrichten, a daily Austrian newspaper. The Jackal looked up from the paper and subtly nodded.

The Jackal stepped into the road and shadowed the three men as they passed his position.

Three blocks farther, after a turn onto a less popular street, Digger gave the all-clear command. "Street's empty. Everyone get ready. Ten feet ahead, Sarge. Red doorway on your left."

With those words, Sarge slipped into the deeply arched doorway and disappeared. The nicely dressed man who unwittingly walked behind Sarge paid no attention as two men quickly approached from behind.

They made no sound.

Troy closed the gap between himself and the target, as did the Jackal. While at that moment, a white cargo van pulled up the curb, and the door suddenly opened.

The target reacted to the noise to his right and turned as the van came to a sudden stop with a slight chirp of the tires.

As the door slid open, Sarge rushed from his hiding spot in the arched doorway and quickly took five large strides toward the target. By the time he reached the man, Troy was behind him as well.

Troy slipped the hood on the target effortlessly in one fluid motion as Sarge grabbed the man's arms in a tremendous, vice-like grip similar to a python subduing its prey. Troy grabbed the man's pants, near the rear belt loop with one hand as his other hand gripped the scruff of the man's neck under the hood.

Together Troy and Sarge had the man, who weighed all of one hundred fifty pounds, soaking wet, off his feet and into the air. A fraction of a second later, they tossed the startled man into the open side door of the van. Harrison Colins, who everyone called Harry or Doc, caught the target mid-air and instantly dropped him to the cold steel floor of the vehicle in a single motion. Troy, Sarge, and the Jackal jumped inside the vehicle as the Jackal slid the van door shut. Jesús

Soto, the final member of the six-man team, mashed the gas pedal to the floor as the van lurched forward and sped away.

It was all over in a few seconds, with no witnesses to the snatch.

As the van departed the empty street and gained speed, a dull silence returned to the peaceful residential area.

With the hooded man pressed to the floor, Harry stuck a syringe into the man's neck and pushed the stopper all the way down. The target's body convulsed for a second, then relaxed as the warm liquid flowed into his bloodstream. Immediately, he drifted off into an unconscious state.

Three blocks later, the van pulled to the side of the boulevard. Digger jumped into the passenger seat as the vehicle sped off and disappeared into the labyrinth of streets.

# 2

## SPANNBERG, AUSTRIA

It was a thirty-five-minute drive to the safe house in Spannberg, located northeast of Vienna. Jesús followed all traffic ordinances since a run-in with the Austrian police force might turn disastrous.

An hour later, Arjun Shakir awoke. Even though they felt like weights held them down, he opened his eyelids. Heavy darkness pervaded everything. As Arjun reached for his head, he found both his arms to be bound. Because of the restraints, he could not reach higher than his chest. Unsure where he was or what was going on, he screamed a rapid-fire, frantic scream. His chest heaved, and his body quivered.

A powerful hand pressed against his mouth. As he twisted in his chair, a deep voice said, "Shhhhhh …" in his left ear.

Arjun's words came out in a panicked tone as the pressure on his mouth abated. "Who … are … you? Where … am … I?" A gasp filled the void between each word.

"Be quiet, Arjun."

"I'm a banker. I have money," Arjun said with a whimper.

"We know who you are."

"I can pay you whatever …"

"We don't want your dirty money, you piece of shit," the voice said.

"Then what do you want?"

"The girl."

"What girl?"

"That's enough talking for now, Arjun."

"But I know nothing about a girl ..."

He felt something cool pressed against his temple, and the distinctive click of the hammer shut him up in mid-sentence.

"I said ... shut ... the hell ... up!" The voice proclaimed in an even sterner and drawn-out manner. "Don't make a sound."

Arjun reached his limit and involuntarily urinated all over himself. The warm liquid ran down the chair in a constant stream onto the floor. A puddle formed around his feet.

"Dammit, Arjun," the voice said.

Something firm smacked him on the back of the head. The force lurched him forward.

"Now we're gonna have to clean that piss up!"

Arjun whimpered, but the sound only caused the barrel to be pressed harder into his temple. It hurt.

"No words. No sounds." The voice was clearly irritated.

Arjun nodded. It finally sunk in.

"Next time you need to take a leak, don't piss all over yourself. We'll take you to the bathroom. Do you understand?" An awkward pause ensued. "Nod your head yes if you understand."

Arjun nodded. He got it.

The voice continued, "We have a long trip ahead, and you need to eat."

A plate was placed on his damp lap.

"I'm going to loosen your bounds, right hand only. You can use it to eat, and that's it. The food is halāl so you can eat it without religious concerns."

Arjun's facial expressions changed.

"Yes, we know all about you, Arjun Shakir, every last detail. If you try to remove the blindfold, I'll put a bullet into your skull and send pieces of your head all over the wall. You got that?"

Arjun proved to be a quick study and simply nodded. His desire to live superseded any thoughts he may have of removing the blindfold. With his right hand freed, he hesitated.

"Eat it," the voice said in a harsh tone. "Now."

Slowly, he reached for whatever rested on his lap. With his eyes covered, he only had his free hand to reach for and feel the contents of the plate. His stomach churned from his nerves, but he forced himself to eat one bite after another, not knowing what would happen if he refused.

Arjun ate in silence. He heard sounds in the distance but could not make out specific voices or words. When he finished, he waited.

Several minutes later, the familiar voice returned and asked, "Are you done?"

He nodded.

"Good," came the reply.

His right hand was bound again. Then he felt a sharp poke in his neck. Something warm entered his body, and all went dark.

# 3

## AUSTRIA

### SAFE HOUSE

Troy confirmed Arjun was unconscious before he turned to his team. The men gathered around the chair, which contained the slumped-over body. All eyes were on their captain.

Troy spoke in a firm yet measured tone. "Okay, guys, I had Doc increase the dosage, so he should be out for about four hours. Pack everything we brought since we need to leave for the airport in under forty-five minutes. Wheels up in less than two hours." With those words, he turned and looked back at Arjun.

The five men in the room all acknowledged the orders.

"And oh," Troy pivoted back to the team. "Someone needs to clean him up. We can't leave him in those piss-dripping clothes." Troy drew in a deep breath. His face contorted. "Plus, it smells like he might have shit himself. Who is gonna step up and be a team player?"

All the heads shook back and forth. The universal symbol for *no*. In this case, it was likely, *Hell no*. None of them wanted to clean up a grown ass man who sat in his own excrement.

"Fine," Troy said, "since none of you will man up, I'll do the deed, but I need help."

Each man took a step back.

"Harry!" Troy's voice came out like a bark as he was unable to hide his frustration.

"Why me?" Harry asked. He turned and glared at the others.

"Because you're the Doc!" Troy said in a firm tone.

"Yes, the doctor, not the damn nurse's aide. Sorry, I don't clean up piss and shit for a living, Cap."

"That's right, you don't, Doc. But as our certified medical professional, you drew the short end of the stick on this one. So, today you do."

"This stinks," Harry said.

"Literally. And trust me, I don't want to wipe a grown man's ass any more than you do. Hell, I don't even like wiping my own ass. But in this case, it needs to be done. I'm not smelling his stank for God knows how many hours once we leave here."

From the other side of the room, the Jackal snickered.

Troy frowned. "And it looks like the Jackal just got put on clean-up duty."

"Me?" The Jackal was unable to hide his incensed response.

"Yes, you! Scrub that piss off the floor and chair until it's clean enough to eat off of. And then dispose of his clothes once Doc and I are done."

The Jackal grimaced.

Troy yelled, "We have a lot of work to do in a short amount of time, so all of you get your asses in high gear!"

# 4

# Vienna International Airport (VIE)

At precisely 11:45 p.m. local time, a white Ford cargo van pulled next to a Gulfstream business jet parked near the executive hangars of the Vienna International Airport.

Jesús, Harry, Digger, and the Jackal exited the van and loaded all their gear into the cargo hold of the plane. With the gear on board, Sarge and Troy carried Arjun inside the jet. Upon entering the sleek aircraft, they turned sideways just to make it down the narrow aisle. Sarge secured Arjun in a seat using a combination of flex cuffs and zip ties. Nothing super fancy, but the restraints would keep him in place for the duration of the flight.

Both pilots, who steadily got things ready for departure from the cockpit, worked for the agency. They knew the drill and didn't ask questions. The pilot and co-pilot were the same two men that flew the team into Vienna two days before.

With Arjun in place, Harry and Digger deplaned and pulled the cargo van off the tarmac, parking it in the lot behind the hangar. They methodically wiped down the vehicle and walked back to the jet. The hum of the engines breached the silence of the night.

As they boarded, another man approached the plane from the shadows. He had an air about him, a purpose in each step. The man paused at the base of the steps and glanced around before he confidently climbed the airstairs. All six men who were getting settled inside the jet turned as he entered.

"Colonel," Troy remarked with a wide smile on his face.

Troy reached out his hand, which Colonel William S. Marshall shook with a vice-like grip.

"Cap," the colonel said as he released his hand. Then he looked at the others sprinkled throughout the fuselage. "Omegas," he said in a deep voice.

In unison, the five men replied, "Colonel."

The colonel smiled and glanced sideways at Troy. "That sound never gets old." He surveyed the plane and immediately focused on the slumped body in the rear seat. "Good job, fellas. I followed your progress and listened in on the comms. For six guys with no prior surveillance training, I was impressed with how cleanly you executed the snatch. No one knows we have him, so let's get Arjun out of Austria. We have a team in place to begin the interrogation. Time is of the essence gentlemen. After all, a young woman's life is at stake."

Everyone took their seats as the pilot announced they would be airborne as soon as air traffic control provided final clearance.

That's when things went south.

The pilot received a call from the tower, and he left the cockpit to make his way back to the team. He paused and cleared his throat. "Colonel, we may have a problem."

"What is it?" Colonel Marshall had a distinct frown on his face.

"A customs and immigration officer is on their way. He says he needs to board and inspect the plane before we can get final clearance."

"Dammit." The colonel shook his head. "I thought at this time of night we could get away without bureaucratic red tape."

"We knew this might happen," Troy said. "Don't worry. We're ready for this, sir." He turned around in his seat. "Get those passports the agency provided us, Harry."

The pilot spoke up as he saw the figure walk across the tarmac. "The officer will be here in sixty seconds." He gestured toward the window with his head.

"Oh man," Digger remarked. "Someone pull Arjun's hood off his head."

"And the blindfold as well," Troy said. "Plus, cut the flex cuffs."

"I'm on it!" Harry darted from his seat towards the slumping body two rows behind him.

"We're gonna tell customs our boy here is sleeping one off?" the Jackal asked.

"Actually," Troy pointed toward the back of the aisle. "Grab a beer from the galley, open it, pour a little into his mouth, then stick the bottle between his legs."

"Good idea," Jesús said. He went to the back of the plane, quickly finished the task, and sat in the open seat across from Arjun just as the immigration and customs officer stepped inside the fuselage.

The man looked exhausted and was obviously in a bad mood based on the scowl spread across his face. "Pazzportz," he growled in a thick Austrian accent. He sounded like Arnold Schwarzenegger, but the pitch in his voice was slightly higher than the famous actor, champion bodybuilder, and former governor of California.

The men handed the passports forward as silence filled the space, the only sound being the hum of the jet's idling engines.

The immigration officer held the stack in his hand and flipped through them meticulously as he made eye contact with each man. His eyes darted from the passport to the men who sat scattered around the interior of the plane.

"Vhat is hiz problem?" asked the officer as he motioned to the man slumped over in the last row. He looked down at the passport and back at the unconscious man.

"Had too much to drink," the colonel said. As he said this, he stuck his outstretched thumb to his lips and moved his hand in an upward motion, like he was throwing back a stiff drink.

"He lewks dead. Not zleeping."

"Oh, gawd no. That's my financial advisor." The colonel raised his voice but remained calm. "He better not be dead since he controls all my money. He just had a few too many. We hit up the bars in Wieden before heading to the airport, and he lost our game of quarter shots. He'll be fine and sleep it off on our flight west."

The immigration officer moved down the aisle and reached out to check for Arjun's pulse. Next, he smelled his breath. "Ugg. He stinkz. Vat is thez quarter shotz?" He turned and went back to the front of the plane, giving each man a sneer as he walked by each aisle.

"Never mind," the colonel said. "Just an American drinking game."

"Purpoz ov trip?"

"Business and a little bit of pleasure." The colonel smiled wide as he made eye contact with the officer. "I own a technology company. Flew in to discuss an acquisition with my executive leadership team." He moved his arms around to indicate the men behind him who comprised that team.

"Vhat company?" the customs officer asked as he looked around the plane suspiciously.

The colonel had a whole backstory memorized but his mind went blank. He looked down and replied, "Amazon." It was the company featured in the magazine lying atop the side table next to his seat. A rare slip-up for a man so hell-bent on control.

The officer's eyebrows arched upward. He looked down at the magazine which caught his eye, then back at the man before him. He snatched the magazine with his right hand and pushed his pointer finger at the picture. Clearly, the man on the cover was not the person who sat before him. His name was even in bold letters on the front cover.

He jammed his finger repeatedly on the cover. "It sayz Jeff Bezos ownz Amazon." The immigration officer flipped through the stack of passports and found the one belonging to the colonel. His finger poked at the opened passport. "This sayz your name iz not Jeff Bezos."

*Damn.* The colonel screwed up big time and got caught with his hand in the proverbial cookie jar. But he recovered and went all in with the flub. "Jeff's our CEO and gets the lion's share of the attention. Rightfully so, he's brilliant, but I'm the man who runs the day-to-day operations. I call the shots from the shadows. You could say Jeff works for me."

The official looked skeptical. His eyes narrowed as he tried to process what he had heard. After a few tense seconds, he nodded his head up and down. "I zee."

"Good, then we can go now?" Colonel Marshall asked.

"No!" the official replied in a curt tone.

"Excuse me?"

The customs official rubbed his thumb against his extended pointer and middle finger. "Long dayz, very strezzful, veey need to check thiz out in vorning. You stay herz tonight." A wicked grin replaced his wearied grimace.

Colonel Marshall shook his head and smiled in return. The customs official might be a crook and a prick, but he wasn't dumb. The colonel reached into his pocket and withdrew a large stack of bills. He whipped off the clean, crisp Benjamins, one at a time.

"Let's see, there are ten of us, including my pilots. I think three hundred each should clear up any misunderstanding. I'll even throw in an extra five hundred if you get the hell off my plane right now. Agreed?"

The man's eyes lit up as the colonel slapped the hundred-dollar bills onto the side table. The officer had hustled many execs over the years, but it rarely brought in more than a thousand euros. "Ves, ves, that vill do juzt fine."

"Good." The colonel handed the man the stack of thirty-five crisp new hundred dollar bills. "On your way then. Have a good night, sir."

"Gewd night," said the official as he walked off the plane without turning back, his pocket much fuller than when he climbed the airstairs a few minutes before.

Troy tilted his head toward the colonel. "Jeff Bezos, huh? I don't recall that being part of our cover story."

The colonel grinned. "Shit happens, Cap. And senior moments occur even to the best of us. But I recovered, and it wasn't a complete disaster."

"Good," Troy said. "Cause if it didn't work, I was gonna drug him and throw him in the back with Arjun."

The colonel laughed. "I'm sure that conscience of yours would have prevented that from occurring."

"We'll never know. Now will we?" Troy replied with his head tilted and a sly grin on his face.

The Jackal raised his hand. "I really think for five hundred more, it would have been really worth it for him to say *Get To The Choppa* in full Governator accent before he departed."

Troy smirked. "For once, you have a good idea, numnuts."

"I try and keep you boys entertained."

"We have clearance to depart," the pilot said through the open cockpit door.

"Thanks," the colonel said as he turned his head. "Now, one of you put Arjun's blindfold and hood back on. Plus, don't forget to flex cuff his wrists. He'll probably wake up before the plane lands."

Four minutes later, the jet rocketed down the runway. As the sleek airplane lifted off the ground, the colonel stood and looked at The Omega Group guys scattered around the interior of the plane. "Wheels up, gentlemen. Now the fun really begins."

# PART II - THE ANGUISH

# 5

## BLACK SITE

### MEDITERRANEAN SEA

At two a.m. (GMT+2), the G650 touched down on a remote island in the middle of the Mediterranean Sea.

Only a speck of an island located between Sicily and Tunisia it was a short flight from Austria. The fact that the island was isolated, sparsely populated, and only slightly developed made it the perfect location for a secret facility that technically didn't exist, at least not according to the United States of America.

In 2002, an international conglomerate leased several hundred acres in the northwest portion of the island directly from the Italian government. The secretive lease agreement paid an exorbitant amount of money each year to the Italians with one stipulation: *Don't ask any questions.* Each year, the funds arrived, and Italy acted like that portion of the island didn't exist.

It was all a ruse.

Without a formal airport because of the tiny population, a large mining operation owned a significant chunk of the island and built a modern airstrip large enough to land 737s during the 1970s. The mining operation went out of business, and the airstrip fell into disrepair but still saw minimal use from time to time, primarily by charter airlines or the occasional private jet.

After the United States built its secret facility, planes frequently landed in the dead of night. Locals never saw what went on within the remote property and only heard the sound of the planes as they landed. Those citizens who mustered up the courage and asked questions about the mysterious comings and goings received visits from the local magistrate, which never went well for the person who asked the question. After a while, the inquiries ceased. The local population got the message. That part of the island was off-limits.

*Hear no evil, see no evil, speak no evil.*

None of the locals or anyone in the Italian government had any idea what really occurred at the northwest tip of the island, and those who operated the secret facilities made sure that the veil of secrecy remained in place.

———◦———

Stepping off the plane, Troy and Sarge departed last. Arjun, now fully awake, reluctantly shuffled between them with his ankles shackled together. The hood over his head, nor the blindfold, was not really necessary since it was so dark. He couldn't have seen anything if he tried. After Sarge barked a few harsh words into his ear, Arjun picked up his pace and followed their instructions.

Two black SUVs waited by the side of the plane. They loaded Arjun into the rear car, sandwiched between Troy and Sarge. Four heavily armed men occupied the vehicle as well. The lead SUV held the colonel and the rest of The Omega Group.

The vehicle sped away as the occupants remained silent. It was less than a two-mile drive from the remote runway to the string of five concrete dome-shaped buildings that lined the base of a long-dormant volcano. Not much was visible since the largest portion of the facilities remained hidden underground. The entire facility had an Area 51 vibe about it, and like the secret base in Nevada, nobody spoke about what really went on within the secure walls.

During the day, the concrete structures looked ominous, like something out of a Cold War-era novel, but in the dead of night, there was nothing to see.

Several men awaited The Omega Group as they arrived. The person who appeared in charge stood closest to the vehicles as they came to an abrupt stop, the tires grinding on the gravel. Colonel Marshall climbed out first. He appeared to recognize the man closest to the vehicle and approached him with a stoic look and outstretched hand.

"Mr. Smith, good to see you once again," the colonel said as he shook the man's hand.

"Likewise, Mr. Smith," replied the tall man with a lean physique. "The room is ready just as you requested, sir."

"Good."

"Mr. Smith?" The Jackal poked Digger in the ribs as they fell in line a few steps behind the colonel.

Digger shrugged. "I don't get it."

"Everyone here is called Mr. Smith," Harry said. "I heard the colonel and Cap talking about it. The generic titles keep up the secrecy and such. You know, James Bond-level shit and all."

"Makes them kinda sound like douches." Digger had a wide smile as he uttered the last part.

"They can do whatever 007 stuff they want," the Jackal said. "I just hope there's a Mrs. Smith on the premises."

"Oh yeah," Digger smiled wide. "The early 2000's Angelina Jolie was smokin' hot." He rolled his eyes. "Until ..."

"The crazy always overtakes," the Jackal laughed. "I know all about those loco chicas. They're good at some stuff, real good in fact, but you always pay the piper one way or the other."

"Zip it!" the colonel turned and pointed at Digger followed by the Jackal. He stood ten paces ahead of the men. The stern glance mean enough to crack glass.

Mr. Smith, the guy who ran the facility, continued to speak to the colonel. "We have briefed the interrogator. He realizes the delicate nature of the situation."

"Good to hear. My men are tired. It's been a long day."

"We have accommodations for you and your team."

"Copy that."

"Follow me," Mr. Smith gestured with his hands as the Omegas moved away from the two vehicles and approached the concrete structures. They passed through the solid steel doors of the building and started down a narrow, gray-colored hallway that went on for quite a way.

After several turns, Mr. Smith stopped and pointed at Troy and Sarge. "Your prisoner goes in here."

They guided Arjun, who sounded like he was about to hyperventilate under the hood, into the room which looked like a typical interrogation room. The kind you'd see on any police show. A four-by-six steel table with two opposing chairs were the only objects in the room. On the far wall was an oversized mirror, no doubt a two-sided one, where others could observe.

Troy and Sarge used the handcuffs and shackles provided and restrained Arjun's hands to the table and his feet to the floor.

On the way out, Troy paused and pressed his mouth up to the side of the hood. "You better answer their damn questions, Arjun, or the time you spend with us is gonna seem like Club Med compared to the hell this outfit will put you through." He paused and said with a chuckle, "Have fun with the sharks. Don't let them bite you."

Arjun shuddered at his words before Troy left the interrogation room with Sarge.

With Arjun secured, Mr. Smith led the six Omega Group members down another long hallway and into another building that served as a bunkhouse. He told the men to make themselves at home.

Inside the spacious area, there was a series of rooms connected by one common room. The beds appeared comfortable, with enough for each man to have his own private room. Set up like an apartment, the bunkhouse included a fully stocked pantry, a media room that included a library of DVDs, and even a game room with a pool table. Exhausted, the men forewent food and showers for sleep as none of the guys had slept in over thirty-six hours.

The colonel didn't join them in the bunkhouse. Instead, he stayed behind with the prisoner and the other, "Mr. Smith."

Troy told the men to each grab a room and get some "rack time." He didn't have to suggest it twice. All six men split off into their own private rooms. The doors closed, and an eerie silence filled the space.

"Aww, hell no!" The Jackal's voice echoed from the end of the hall a minute after his door slammed shut.

Cap opened his door and peeked out. "What is it now, loudmouth? Forget to pack your sex toys?"

"Someone's gotta switch rooms with me, Cap," bellowed the Jackal whose door swung wide open.

"And why is that?"

"The bedspread in my room, it's the exact one she, who shall not be named, had at her place. I can't sleep in that damn room. I'll have Lorena Bobbitt nightmares all night long."

"Which ex?" Sarge asked. He heard the commotion and poked his head into the hall. "There's quite the laundry list of crazies to choose from when it comes to yours truly."

"Yeah, about as long as my Johnson," the Jackal said.

"Well, maybe the list ain't that long after all," Sarge retorted. He was unable to let out a loud laugh after he uttered the last few words.

The Jackal shot Sarge the bird. "The one who had a car movie named after her."

Sarge rubbed his chin. "Oooh, that one. Damn. I take it all back. They are all at least a little bit crazy, but that one took it to a new level."

"Uh, yeah," the Jackal said.

"Wait, is that the one who went to the weirdo naturalist and made you hold a stick of butter in your hand, swung the pendulum thing over the butter, then said you had a dairy allergy?" Troy asked.

"The one and only," the Jackal rolled his eyes. "Bat shit, meet crazy."

"Whew," Cap let out a long sigh. "That one was some sort of special right there."

"Come on. Help a brother out, Cap. I can't fall asleep in this room."

"Well, I'm not sleeping in that room either. It's probably all voodoo or something."

"Actually, I think the naturalists' practices were more aligned with wiccan concepts and not voodoo. To be precise." Digger's voice bellowed from the other side of his closed door.

"Well, whatever it is, it's whack in my book," Sarge said.

"I'm not going to get in a discussion on holistic healing methods tonight, so you all need to shut the hell up cause my ass needs to go catch some zzz's." Digger grew quiet.

Troy pointed at the Jackal, then down the hall toward the game room. "Nice leather couch next to the pool table has your name all over it if you can't get past the bedspread, dude."

"Thanks, Cap." The sarcasm was evident in the Jackal's voice. "Thanks a lot."

"Make better choices when it comes to chicks in the future," Troy said as he closed his door.

"Amen to that," Sarge added. "Those are words all of us can live by."

The Jackal made a guttural grunt sound, retreated to the room, and came back out with a sheet and pillow a minute later. He begrudgingly headed down the hall toward the leather couch. "Thanks for nothing, dickwads." Those were his final words before he crashed on the couch.

# 6

## BLACK SITE

Three individuals stood a few feet away from the double-sided mirror. They watched the prisoner, but none of them said anything.

Only the clicking sound of the vintage-style wall clock disturbed the silence. The antiquated clock reminiscent of something found in schools or government buildings.

With every passing minute, the prisoner shifted in his seat. He appeared fidgety. Several times, he pulled against the restraints. Those motions met with immediate resistance as the metal cuffs tugged against the fixed rings mounted to both the tabletop and the floor.

As the three people observed the prisoner, a knock reverberated from the door behind them.

"Enter." The person standing in the middle of the three turned towards the door.

Colonel Marshall stepped into the darkened room.

"Sir." The man in the middle said as the other two on either side of him just nodded.

"We about ready?" The colonel asked as his gaze bounced between the three people before him, moving from left to right.

"Yes, we are." The man to the far right said. He wore a white dress shirt, with sleeves rolled up past his elbows, and dark navy-blue pants paired with brown loafers.

The colonel looked back and forth at the three people in front of him and nodded. "Who will conduct the interrogation?"

The man on the right said, "I will, sir."

Colonel Marshall watched the man for several awkward seconds. His gaze went from the brown loafers all the way up to the man's face. "And I take it you have a high degree of skill extracting intel?"

"I always get what is needed, sir."

*Huh*, the sound slipped out of the colonel's lips. "In my experience, interrogators cannot guarantee success."

The man in the middle cleared his throat. "That's correct, always is not a term we use lightly in these situations."

"This man in custody is not a member of Al-Qaeda or the Taliban. He's weak and scared. I'll break him, sir."

"We don't need him broke. Anyway, sometimes those who look the most pathetic and disheveled surprise you." The colonel stopped. "At least in my experience. Underestimating one's enemy is the quickest way to meet a premature demise."

"Noted, sir. I'll get what you need in a timely fashion."

"We need actionable intel, and we don't have time to dick around." The frustration in the colonel's voice grew stronger with each word. "Your team came highly recommended. I pray I have not placed my trust in the wrong hands."

With both hands raised, the man in the middle spoke in a reassuring voice. "We know what's at risk, sir. And we know time is of the essence. What my colleague meant to say is that we've read the file and studied the prisoner's bio. We will get you what you need so you can continue your operation."

The frown displayed on the colonel's face revealed his irritation. "Get in there and get it done. I don't need to remind any of you what is at risk if you don't." He didn't wait for a response. His body pivoted, and he turned and left the room.

The man in the middle turned to the person dressed in the white shirt and blue pants. "You heard him. Get started."

"Roger that, Mr. Smith."

When the hood and blindfold was pulled forcefully off Arjun's head, a bright light greeted his petrified eyes. It took a minute before he adjusted to the bombardment of white light. Tears flowed down his exposed cheeks as the illumination took hold of his opened eyes.

"Arjun Shakir?" The gruff voice boomed directly behind him.

"Yes," replied Arjun. He trembled and his voice cracked.

"Welcome to hell." The voice spoke in a detached tone.

"Help me, Allah!" Arjun cried out. Despair hung in the air with each word. His voice was pitiful, the fear palpable.

"Your God can't help you in here," the man in the brown loafers said. "You're all alone, and your ass is mine until you give me what I require."

For the second time in less than a day, a stream of warm liquid ran down his leg and pooled on the floor as Arjun pissed himself involuntarily.

**7**

**BLACK SITE**

After a prolonged period of sleep deprivation, Troy crashed hard at the bunkhouse and got solid sleep. It turned out to be a longer stretch of interrupted sleep than he had in a while; it wasn't enough, but he couldn't complain. After all, while on a mission, there's never enough sleep. It comes in spurts but is never truly what your body needs.

Once he woke up, Troy made his way to the main building. After several turns he found room 124 and pounded his fist on the door. The repetitive motion jarred the entryway. The wooden door shook with the force exerted by his powerful strikes.

"Enter," a voice said from the other side of the thick door.

Troy stepped inside. The sparse room only contained a steel table with two sets of chairs that faced each other.

The interrogator looked up from the papers in front of him. "Yes? Can I help you?"

"Hope so. Where are we at with Arjun, bossman?" Troy pulled out a chair from the table and spun it around. The legs scraped against the floor and made a sound like fingernails down a chalkboard. He winced slightly at the sound but sat down across from the interrogator.

The man ignored Troy's question and instead continued to look at the notes in front of him. A few seconds of awkward silence fell between them before he closed the files and glanced up. "And you are?" he asked.

"My men call me Cap. And you?"

"Around this facility, I'm known as Harvey."

Harvey sat upright with no visible slouch. His broad shoulders pushed back toward the chair. Gray streaks ran through his thick, black hair, giving off a distinguished salt-and-pepper look. His weathered face contained crow's feet around his eyes, which indicated he had spent many years under a blazing sun. Harvey had a sharp nose and chiseled jaw that most would find intimidating.

But not Troy, who merely smirked at the man's name. "Harvey, huh? As in the big white rabbit?"

Harvey smiled. "I would think a Jimmy Stewart movie was a little before your time, young man."

"Looks can be deceiving. My pops and I watched old movies together all the time growing up. Every Friday after he got home, we downed a large pizza and watched movies till we fell asleep on the couch. He especially loved Jimmy Stewart. Hollywood doesn't make actors like that anymore."

"No, no, they don't."

Troy glanced down at his watch. "I've asked once, Harvey, and I don't enjoy asking again. Where are you with Arjun? How long until we get our intel?"

"I already cracked him wide open, Cap."

"What?" Troy asked in an incredulous tone.

"Arjun was one of the easier ones they gave me in a long time. He told me everything he knew and then some."

"Then why the hell are we still here? A young girl's life depends on what Arjun knows, for Christ's sake." The irritation was impossible to hide in Troy's voice.

"I'm well aware of what is at risk, Cap," Harvey replied. "Just because I know I broke him doesn't mean I'm right. I rarely allow what I'm told during the first session to be the gospel truth. I'll let Arjun rest a little longer and then hit him hard again, metaphorically speaking, that is, and see if his story changes."

"When will you start back and confirm what he told you?" asked Troy anxiously.

Harvey looked at his watch. "Eighteen minutes." He tapped his timepiece with his index finger. "Arjun has been sleeping for a little over an hour. What I did drained him of everything he had. He needed some rest. It should take me less than an hour once I wake him up. As long as Arjun is forthright, it should go quickly. Mr. Smith should be able to brief your team as soon as I'm done. Then you and your men can be on your way."

Troy pressed him. "Tell me, does he know where the girl is?"

"You'll know soon enough."

"Look, Harvey, this is ..."

Harvey cut him off and snapped his fingers. "Hey, listen here, Cap ... don't tell me how to do my job cause I sure as hell wouldn't do that to you. Let me do what I do best. You'll have your intel soon enough. I'm not dragging my feet here. Not trying to be difficult. My methods work, but I must be sure what I provide you is spot on. I'm fully aware of what is at stake." He paused for a moment before he added, "Deal?"

Troy thought for a moment and knew he was wrong to question Harvey's expertise. He swallowed his pride and said, "You're right, Harvey. Sorry, I snapped."

With a warm smile, Harvey put his hands out in a de-escalating manner. "No offense, Cap. You have skin in the game, and I respect that. I'll get you what he knows once I'm sure he's not full of shit."

"And you'll know that how?" Troy asked.

"Let's just say it's an acquired skill to become a human lie detector. There are subtle ways I can tell if someone is lying to me. Ticks, mannerisms, and even vocal inflection really run the gamut and are highly specific to each person they bring to me. That's why it's not a quick process. I must establish a baseline to build off. Been doing this a long time, and I have a good sense when someone is straight up versus trying to snow job me. I'm sure what you do is no different. Experience often breeds wisdom."

"I can respect that," Troy said.

Several moments passed without words.

"Look. We might have got off on the wrong foot. So, Cap, what is your real name? If I can be so bold as to ask."

"Troy, Troy Evans."

Harvey's expression changed; his hardened features softened. He appeared surprised by the name that was uttered. "As in Green Beret Captain Troy Evans?"

"Guilty as charged." Troy sat back and folded his arms. His eyebrows raised slightly before he added, "Have we met before?"

"No, but I've heard a lot about you."

"From whom?" Troy asked, the curiosity clear in his voice.

Instead of answering, Harvey stood from the chair, leaned over, and extended his hand over the stainless-steel table.

The action surprised Troy, but he stood as well and shook Harvey's hand. Both men had exceptionally powerful grips.

"It's rare you get to meet a real honest-to-goodness American hero," Harvey said in a firm tone.

"The hell you say. Trust me, Harvey, I'm no hero." Troy looked somewhat embarrassed as he sat back in his chair. The handshake and statement caught him off guard, which was not a common occurrence.

"The person who told me all about you would beg to differ."

"And who would that be?" Troy asked.

"Dawson Phillips."

The name startled Troy. Now he knew why Harvey called him a hero. Troy commanded Dawson in his previous unit. He saved Dawson's life during an operation that became almost mythical among the Special Forces community.

Operation Lightning Bolt.

"Wow, I've not heard that name in a while. And how do you know Dawson?"

"He's my nephew."

"No shit? Guess it really is a small world after all." Troy's mind went back to the operation that almost cost Dawson and most of the team, including Troy, their lives. Troy suddenly felt at ease with Harvey. The connection they shared allowed him to talk freely, which was not the norm for him.

"How is he?" Troy asked. "It's been a minute since we've talked."

Harvey smiled warmly. "Dawson is good. He has good days amongst the bad, but he's on an upward trend and speaks of you often."

"He was a good soldier with a big heart. I miss our chats late at night. Dawson always had something to discuss, and even if you disagreed with every word he uttered, somehow, you would see his side by the end of the conversation. I was sad to see him leave the Army soon after our last mission went all to hell."

"You know warfare, Troy. Operators are wound tight, and sometimes when that spool of thread unravels, there's no getting it back to how it was. He's a lot quieter now after he got out."

"I understand how that goes."

"But he has a new job in Knoxville, even met a girl he's settled down with. They are talking about starting a family."

"Good for him," Troy smiled. "I'm happy to hear he's doing well. Everyone deserves a chance at happiness."

"You're his hero. You know that, right?"

"Look, Harvey, I'm proud to have Dawson think so highly of me, but like I already said, I'm no hero ..."

"Yes, I know, I know. You just do your job. Nothing more, nothing less. Dawson told me about your humility."

"It's not humility, Harvey. It's the truth. Anyway, I've always believed that genuine heroes never make it back home. We bury some in unmarked graves, others at cemeteries around the world, or even in sacred locations like Arlington."

"I respectfully disagree," Harvey said. "There might only be a few, but we have walking, talking heroes amongst us."

Troy ignored the compliment aimed in his direction. "Give my best to Dawson next time you talk to him. Tell him to call me sometime. I owe him a Guinness one of these days. It's been too long, and we need to catch up. In fact, if you have a pen, I can give you my number and email address if you would like. Although, I must admit I'm rarely stateside to answer the phone. I do most of my communication via email nowadays."

Harvey pushed a pen across the stainless steel table and tossed a pad of sticky notes in Troy's direction.

Troy scribbled down his contact info and slid the pen and pad back to Harvey.

"The rumors were that you got out," Harvey said. "No longer part of Special Ops."

"Well, I'm here, aren't I?"

"I even tried looking you up at Dawson's request last year. Got nowhere trying to track you down with the Army brass. One person told me you moved over to the agency and worked for the Special Activities Center."

"Not the case. I'm still in the Army and still in Special Ops. It's just that." Troy paused and took a moment to consider his next words. "Let's just say they reassigned me, and my new group falls outside the typical purview of the big Army hierarchy."

"Black ops?"

"I didn't say that." Troy shrugged and did little to contain a wry smile.

"Your new group have a designation?"

"Classified," remarked Troy in a coy tone. "You know the drill."

"Sure do," Harvey said as he motioned with his outstretched arms. "According to the United States military, this facility doesn't exist. Neither do the countless others littered throughout the world. The government loves plausible deniability. Unfortunately, they also require answers with ever-changing and expedited frequency. Hence why these facilities still exist. Unofficially, of course."

"At least you're not in Diego Garcia. That place is really in the middle of nowhere."

Harvey nodded. "Yup, know all about that place. I spent three months of my life there last year. You've been?"

Troy's eyebrows raised before he replied. "Once or twice."

The two men carried on like they had known each other for years.

"Do you like being an interrogator?" Troy asked.

"I do. And I'm damn good at it if I do say so myself."

"No issues with ..." Troy hesitated before he chose his words carefully, "the methodologies you use on those you extract intel from?"

"Are you implying we torture our guests here at this facility?" asked Harvey with a quizzical look. "Or use enhanced interrogation techniques?"

"Well, don't you?"

"Not me, but I can't say it never happens here or at other places. Speaking only for myself, I've found over the years that psychological methodologies work better than anything that could be construed as physical torture. I like to call what I put my subjects through as mental anguish. It allows me to extract valuable intel in a timely manner."

"And if you can't break them using your mental anguish tactics?"

"That's not a common occurrence. Every person has their breaking point."

"But what happens when your practices don't work?" Troy asked. "Nobody hits a thousand in this line of work."

"If I can't extract what is needed, then I bring in someone else who may have better luck."

"And what methods do they use?" Troy asked.

Harvey shrugged. "I can only speak for myself, not others."

"That's a deflection."

"Speaking of not wanting to answer questions. You ever lose sleep over the people you've killed, Captain Evans?"

"What is this sleep you speak of?"

"Touché. And you claim I use deflection."

"No, Harvey, I don't," Troy said.

"Really? How so?"

"Well, I haven't killed as many as some might think. But, the men I have ushered into the afterlife deserved what they got. We didn't run around Kabul or Ramadi shooting random civilians. Our targets were precise, verified hostiles. On the off chance, I've encountered an asshole with a gun along the way who tried to do harm to my men or myself, I've acted accordingly. My conscience is clean. Men with clean consciences sleep soundly, in my experience. And I sleep like an absolute rock, at least when I can actually get some sleep."

Harvey smiled. "Psychopaths sleep soundly as well. At least, according to most clinical psychologists."

"No doubt." Troy nodded. "But I feel confident my actions are on the side of justice. I don't get sent after car thieves or tax cheats. We go after the worst of the worst, and they deserve what's coming. Besides, when our boots are on the ground, I have complete operational authority. If something doesn't pass the smell test, I can pull the plug at any time. Not a privilege one is granted while on missions with the big Army." Troy grew tired of the attention and pivoted. "How about you?"

"In regard to my line of work, I look at it this way. Most people want to eat chicken, but few people will work at the processing plant or raise chickens on their own and break their necks with their bare hands, then chop off their heads. Interrogation is a brutal business and not for the faint of heart. Same thing with the War on Terror. Everybody thinks our government should prevent the next 9/11. However, when it comes to extracting the intel needed, politicians act like weasels. They dodge the hard questions while pontificating how they want us to treat detainees with respect and play by Washington's rule book. They live in make-believe land, while the rest of us operate in a harsh, unforgiving reality. Sometimes reality really does bite. We do what we got to do. That goes for you, and it goes for me."

"You'll get no argument from me on that," Troy said. "So, how long have you been doing this?"

"Thirteen years as an interrogator, thirty-one years with the Army," Harvey said.

"That's a long time. You have a family?"

"Been married for twenty-eight years. First and only marriage."

"That's rare in the service."

"You bet. My wife and I have three grown kids."

"You're gone a lot?"

"I pull ninety-day stretches overseas, then home for the same amount of time before I head back out."

"The family knows what you do?"

Harvey smirked. "My wife has a pretty good idea. That's a hard thing to conceal from someone you sleep next to every night. Plus, she swears to God I talk in my sleep," Harvey said with a chuckle. "But God, I hope not. Who knows what may have slipped out? As for my kids, they just know I'm in Army intelligence. They never really asked, and I never really told."

Troy laughed. "How Bill Clinton of you."

"My version of don't ask, don't tell is slightly different from his," Harvey responded with a hearty laugh. "So, how about you? Married?"

Troy shook his head. "Military life isn't always conducive to having a family, in my opinion, and certainly not with the path I chose. No offense, since it seems to work for you."

"None taken. Like you alluded to, most of my friends are on their second or third marriages. I know I'm beyond blessed to be happily married to number one."

"As for me, it's hard to have a normal relationship when you are gone for a six-to-twelve-month rotation with little notice," Troy said.

"Hmmm, sounds like a lonely existence if you ask me."

"There was someone. But that ship sailed a long time ago."

"Did she marry someone else?" Harvey asked.

"No, nothing like that. She's still single and works for the Bureau in the counterterrorism division."

"And?" Harvey pressed.

"And I made the choice a long time ago for this life instead of that one."

"You make the right call?"

Troy was out of his comfort zone, way outside it. He didn't answer and instead tapped his watch. "I think your eighteen minutes is up, Harvey. Time to get Arjun back in the hot seat and get us what we need."

Harvey looked down at his watch and nodded. The timer he set went off at that exact moment. "Your internal clock is spot on. Why don't you join the rest of the guys, Troy, and get an hour or so more of rest. Maybe grab some chow. For a facility in the middle of nowhere, the food here is phenomenal. I think the chef they hired used to work for U2 and also The Rolling Stones when they were on tour. Or so I heard."

"That must be what kept the Stones alive all these years."

Harvey chuckled. "Nah, I think they made a deal with someone else a long time ago to achieve their longevity."

"No doubt. Thanks for the chat, Harvey. I'll try to get some rest and grub."

"I have a feeling you'll need it soon."

"Always do." Troy stood up and extended his hand outward.

Harvey shook it enthusiastically.

"Thanks for the talk," Troy said. "I respect what you and your team do for our country."

"Ditto, Troy. Ditto."

# 8

## BLACK SITE

Ninety minutes later, an in-depth brief with Mr. Smith, Harvey, and The Omega Group concluded.

The colonel thanked Harvey and Mr. Smith for their efforts, and the two men left the Omegas alone inside the conference room.

"What's next?" Digger asked. "Let's say Arjun is correct. We still don't know the exact spot, and that's a big ass city to search for one little girl. Not a location we have many resources available either. How are we going to initiate a rescue mission to get her before the deadline passes without more detailed intel?"

Before the colonel could answer, there was a knock at the door.

"Enter," the colonel didn't hide his irritation at the interruption.

One of the facility's guards, who appeared out of breath with trickles of sweat rolling down his forehead, stepped into the room. "Sorry to disturb you, sir, but your pilot asked us to deliver this to you." He pulled out a cell phone from his right pocket. "The pilot said it has not stopped ringing for the past ten minutes."

The colonel took the phone, and before he could thank the man for delivering it, the device rang. As he looked down at the screen, his expression changed. "I better take this," he said as he turned to the team. "It's Glenn."

The six men of The Omega Group could only hear one side of the conversation.

"What is it? Glenn, slow down ... take a breath ... did you recognize the voice? Hold on, start from the beginning, and don't leave out a word of what the kidnappers said ..."

For three minutes, the colonel said nothing. Besides a few grunts and sighs, the colonel remained silent.

Troy and the others waited and listened.

Finally, the colonel spoke. "No, I'm not sure it's a good idea ... only bring ten million with you ... you were smart to ask for proof of life. Of course, we can be there within two and a half hours. Call me back when your plane crosses the Atlantic. Stay strong, Glenn. We'll get her back. I promise."

As the call concluded, the colonel fell silent. Lost in his thoughts, he stared at the ground, but said nothing.

Troy pulled him back to the present. "What's going on?"

"The kidnappers." The colonel looked up. "They pushed the date forward. They want half the money delivered tomorrow at noon, or she dies. The physical exchange of her and the rest of the money won't happen until the original deadline."

"Ten million?" Troy asked.

"Yes, in euros." The colonel said.

"Glenn already has the money?"

"Yes."

"Drop location?"

"Paris. At Madame Brasserie, a restaurant on the first platform of the Eiffel Tower."

"I know where it is," Troy said. "Tomorrow at noon?"

The colonel nodded. "Correct."

"Anything else?"

"Yes. If he doesn't come alone, they'll kill her."

"Of course, they said that." Troy sighed as he rolled his eyes. "Just like out of a movie. These guys are amateurs."

"Be that as it may. They have her and they just altered the demands."

"Copy that."

"You familiar with the layout of the tower?" the colonel asked.

"Yes. Been there several times. The first time when I was twelve."

"That was a long time ago, Cap."

"I've been there within the past three years."

The colonel nodded. "Location assessment?"

"That's a tough place for us to operate," Troy said. "We won't be able to ensure Glenn's safety. Too many civilians for my comfort. On the ground would be better. Anywhere in the structure will be a logistics nightmare for our team."

"Any place for Digger to set up shop? Give us an eye in the sky?"

"Not that I recall. But I really need to see the tower to give an accurate assessment."

"If Glenn goes there alone with all that money, they'll kill him," Jesús moved his index finger along his throat in a slow motion from left to right. "And then kill his daughter."

"I agree," Sarge said.

"I would," the Jackal added. "You know, if I was a bad guy."

"Glenn won't be alone, Sarge." Troy looked at Sarge. "I won't allow that. Plus, they won't kill Glenn or the girl."

"You know that how?" the Jackal asked.

"Trust me. They'll want the full twenty ..."

Troy didn't finish. He became lost in his thoughts as he ran scenarios in his head.

The colonel watched and smiled as his men talked back and forth. The efficiency of his team and their problem-resolution skills were something to behold.

"Earth to Cap." Digger snapped his fingers, trying to get Troy out of his daydream.

"Give me a few minutes, guys." Troy stood and walked to the corner of the room.

"I think Cap is formulating a plan," the colonel said.

"Are you?" Harry asked.

"Of course he is. Right, Cap?" the colonel asked.

"Well, I have the start of one," Troy displayed a slight grin as he turned around. "And I think I know how to have a tracker placed on the money that can't be detected if anything goes south."

"We gonna like this plan?" the Jackal asked.

"Do you ever like my plans, numbnuts?"

"Good point, Cap."

"The question is, will Glenn like the plan?" Digger asked.

Troy thought for a moment before he answered. "Probably not."

"Wonderful," Harry said.

"We can discuss Cap's plan on the flight to Paris, fellas. And if anyone has a better idea, I'm all ears," the colonel said. "You guys can figure anything out. I have faith in you."

They all nodded.

"Collect your gear. We won't be coming back here anytime soon." The colonel instructed.

"How about Arjun?" Jesús asked.

"He'll leave tomorrow night and be a guest at the Iron Lady," the colonel said. "Until this whole incident is resolved."

"And then?" Jesús asked.

"Then he'll likely face charges for his part in the kidnapping." The colonel said.

Jesús wiped his brow. "Floating out in the Indian Ocean on board the Iron Lady will make his stay at this place seem like a Disney World vacation."

"Don't do the crime if you can't do the time," Troy said with a slight chuckle.

"You and your dad watch reruns of Baretta growing up, Cap?" the colonel asked.

"All the time." Troy nodded. "All the time ..."

# PART III - The Inducement

# 9

## HOUSTON, TEXAS

Glenn Roberts climbed aboard his private Gulfstream jet, the larger of the two he owned. His right knee ached by the time he reached the fifth step. The stress and his recent physical inactivity had caught up with him.

One of his pilots, Mark Elliott, met him at the top of the airstairs and greeted him with a warm smile and pat on the shoulder. "Great to have you on-board, Mr. Roberts."

"Sorry about the short notice, Mark." Glenn stepped inside the plane as a twinge of pain shot from his knee down to his foot, the result of an old football injury from his college days.

"Not a problem, sir," Captain Elliott said.

Glenn's eyes were bloodshot; he hadn't slept in almost two days. "I need to be in Paris as fast as you can get us there."

Captain Elliott nodded. "I have already filed a flight plan. We'll peel some paint off this bird, Mr. Roberts."

The flight attendant, Amanda, a young woman in her late twenties who had worked for him going on six years, tried to convince Glenn to rest, but sleep eluded him most of the flight. His mind kept agonizing over his daughter, Abigale.

*Had they hurt her further?*

*Would they make good on their threats?*

The youngest of his four children, Abby, as she was affectionately known, became the "oops" child after over twenty years of marriage. Glenn and his wife thought they were past the child-rearing phase of their relationship. His three older children attended college when their younger sister was still in diapers. She was Glenn's baby, his sweet little girl, and he doted on her all the time.

Maybe too much.

In Glenn's eyes, Abby could do no wrong. His older children had experienced the highs and lows of the oil business while growing up. Glenn had made a small fortune many times over and just as quickly lost everything but the shirt on his back. However, things changed when Abby was about three. His business turned good for several years, then phenomenal. When his largest exploratory field hit black gold, the big five oil companies came knocking at his headquarters in Houston. He received an incredible offer to be acquired from one of them, but he politely refused. In fact, Glenn rejected the second offer, then the third, and so on. He rejected almost ten offers over a two year period and was glad he did so. Over that time period, the business valuation increased by almost a hundredfold. Instead of making millions, he netted well over a billion dollars when he finally sold out to big oil. And he smiled all the way to the bank.

While his three older children struggled through college and even had to take out loans, Abby knew of no such hardships. Glenn spoiled her rotten and only saw his little angel every time she asked for something. The older three children loved their little sister but resented her at the same time.

During Abby's senior year of high school, with Glenn pushing into his mid-sixties, Abby decided she wanted to take a gap year and travel abroad before starting college. Hesitant at first, Glenn and his wife tried to talk her out of it, but as usual, what Abby wanted, she got.

Glenn had no way of knowing at the time that letting her go would be the worst decision he had ever made.

As the flight continued its trek to Charles de Gaulle International Airport, Glenn's thoughts drifted back to the moment that rocked his world.

# 10

## One Week Ago

Glenn took his usual break at two p.m. CST. Located across the street from his office building in downtown Houston, the park acted as a sanctuary away from the chaos which encompassed his office. Even though Glenn sold his stake in the oil fields he still maintained a strong presence in the industry. After several minutes of walking, he got tired. The heat and humidity took its toll, and he sat on a green park bench across from a duck pond. The warm sun bore down on his face, and the break felt good. His feet ached. Father Time caught up with him faster than he would have liked. The extra weight he carried did him no good, neither did his eating habits or lack of any measurable exercise.

A man approached and took a seat next to him. Glenn glanced up briefly to see a well-dressed man in a tailored gray suit sitting on the bench to his right. The man had a closely cropped beard and black hair sprinkled with flecks of gray. Within seconds, the man said hello, and Glenn returned the courtesy before he looked away toward the ducks who dotted the water across from where he sat.

After a minute passed, the man spoke. "It's a fine day, isn't it, Mr. Roberts?"

Slightly startled, Glenn turned and locked eyes with the stranger. He didn't recognize the man, but didn't want to come across as rude.

After all, he interacted with lots of people in his line of work, so it was possible they had met at some point.

"Yes, it's a beautiful day, Mr.? Sorry, I can't seem to place where we met before. Remind me again, please."

"We haven't," the man said.

"Oh," Glenn said.

"But I recognize you from the times you have been in magazine articles and on television programs."

Glenn smiled. The ego boost always worked well on him. "Yes, I'm on there from time to time." A moment of silence passed before Glenn asked, "Sorry, I didn't catch your name."

"That's because I didn't offer it" A smile formed on the corner of the man's lips. He leaned toward Glenn and extended his right hand. "My name is Nizar. I work in the oil and gas industry like yourself, except my specialty is in the Middle East."

"Ahh, the big fields."

"Yes, they are quite large."

"And what brings you to Houston? You're a little early for the International Energy Summit. It doesn't start for two more weeks."

"I'm here to see you, actually."

"Me?" Glenn asked. The statement surprised him.

"Yes, you. I have something for you."

Nizar reached into his suit coat and removed a small black box from the inside pocket. The box appeared to be covered on the outside with suede and was about five inches long, one inch wide, and one inch tall.

He looked at the box carefully before handing it over to Glenn. "It's a gift," he replied. "From my employer."

Glenn received the box with a puzzled look. "And who do you work for?"

Nizar ignored the question. "Please open it. It will be an unexpected surprise."

Glenn was very much a control freak and not fond of surprises. However, he slowly opened the top of the box. There were hinges on one side, so the top flipped up and stayed upright.

As he looked inside the box lined with a crimson-red material, his arms involuntarily jerked. Enough so that he almost dropped the box and its contents to the ground in a state of fright. A human finger was inside. A delicate, pale, severed index finger.

"What the hell is this?" Glenn yelled. "Is this someone's idea of a sick joke?"

Then he noticed it, and his mind immediately recognized the ring upon the slender forefinger. There was no mistaking that ring.

Abby's ring.

He knew it well since he had given her the gift for her sweet sixteen birthday. A rare sapphire and diamond ring, one of a kind, made especially for the occasion by one of the finest jewelers in all of New York City. Many Americans could buy a house for the cost of the jewelry.

Realization struck like a sucker punch to the gut. Not only did the ring belong to Abby, but so did the finger.

Glenn's horror turned to rage, like the flip of a switch.

As he turned his eyes away from the box and toward Nizar, he saw the man cradling a gun pointed directly at him.

"Listen to me, Glenn, and listen carefully. For I will not repeat what I am about to tell you."

He had Glenn's undivided attention.

"Yes, that is your daughter's finger, and unless you want to receive various-sized boxes with other parts of her, you will do exactly as I say. Do you understand?"

Glenn's mind swam, his rage hardly controllable. But somehow, he tempered the anger. His years of training at West Point and the Army kicked in.

"Yes," he muttered through gritted teeth. "What the hell do you want?"

"Not much," Nizar said. "Only twenty million dollars!"

"Excuse me!"

"You heard me. I spoke quite clearly. My employer requires twenty million dollars for the safe return of your beloved Abby. That is a drop in the bucket for a man of your wealth."

Glenn seethed. "This is extortion."

"Actually, it's a ransom. You've had many things in this life, and now you have a ransomed daughter, Glenn. We are holding her, have cut off her finger, and will do much worse if you do not acquiesce to our demands. The question now is, what are you going to do?"

There was no question in either man's mind what Glenn would do.

"My employer demands to be paid in euros, not dollars. I'm afraid the US dollar just isn't what it used to be."

"When do I pay it, and how do I get my daughter back?"

Nizar stood, the gun still in his hand, held at his hip and pointed at Glenn. "I will call you with instructions. We fully understand it may take a little time to get twenty million euros. Expect the call in a few days. By the way, my employer wishes to be paid in five hundred euro notes. It will be easier to transport for both of us."

"Uh huh," Glenn muttered.

"We will monitor your movements and all of your electronic devices. If you attempt to notify the authorities, Abby will meet a very slow and very painful demise. We know you are well-connected with the government. If you fail to pay or do not follow our instructions explicitly, we will chop your daughter in little pieces and FedEx her back one box at a time. Do I make myself clear?"

"Perfectly," Glenn said. His hands balled into a fist and slightly trembling. Every fiber of his being wanted to reach out and obliterate the man who stood before him with his bare hands.

"When we call, you will come to the designated exchange spot alone. Understood?"

"Yes," Glenn said.

Nizar took several steps back and slid the gun under the waistband at the small of his back. He let his coat cover the bulge, turned, and left.

Ten feet from the park bench, he paused and turned back. "By the way, I almost forgot. Keep the box and its contents. It's a gesture of our seriousness and resolve. You keep your end of the bargain, and we will keep ours. Abby, thanks you in advance for your cooperation." He then turned away from Glenn and kept walking. As he got to the end of the park, a car was waiting for him. He climbed in and never looked back. The car sped away and out of view within seconds.

Glenn sat motionless at the bench with only his thoughts and a box with the severed finger of his beloved daughter. His mind raced.

*What can I do?*

*Who can I contact if not the authorities?*

Tears flowed down his cheeks as his rage turned to terror.

Several minutes passed before he realized one person could help.

*Him. He's the only one.*

Glenn's mind considered how to contact his old friend with no one knowing. That took longer to deduce.

# 11

## PRESENT DAY

### PARIS, FRANCE

"Soooo this is what ten million dollars looks like?" The Jackal asked. His voice dripped with sarcasm as he picked up a stack of bills and flipped through them in a rapid motion like a card shark breaking in a new deck.

"They're euros, Sherlock." Troy stood a few feet away and paced back and forth across the carpet. "Not greenbacks."

"Dollars, euros, whatever, they spend the same, Cap," the Jackal said.

"It's a lot of dough." Jesús let out a slow whistle.

"I've never seen a five-hundred euro note with my own eyes." Harry grabbed a stack of bills. "Vegas and I could have a little fun right here. Maybe a little too much fun if I brought some buddies along." He smacked the Jackal on the shoulder with the bound bills.

"You'll never find me near that den of iniquity," the Jackal crossed himself but could barely keep a straight face.

Troy pointed towards the heavens. "I'm just waiting for the bolt of lightening to descend from He who sits on high and fry your lying ass."

The Jackal snickered. "Did you know five-hundred euro notes are affectionately known as Bin Laden's, Cap."

"So, I've heard. Used predominately by the criminal elements worldwide. The EU stopped printing them and are supposed to phase them out of circulation down the road."

"How much is the entire stack worth in US dollars?" Sarge asked as he looked at the neat stacks of money on the table before him and simply shook his head in amazement.

Only a few seconds passed before Digger rattled off the value in US dollars.

"Dang! You know that how?" Sarge asked.

"Because he is a genius, Sarge!" Troy exclaimed.

"Remind me why the genius passed up a full ride at MIT to join the Army then?" the Jackal asked.

"To work with you dumbasses, of course." Digger looked at his teammates with a sly grin. "Besides, I'm not really a genius." He held up his smartphone. "I just know how to use one of these. Google knows currency exchange rates in seconds."

"I'm still hung up on the fact you ditched MIT to join the Army. That was a piss poor decision," the Jackal said.

Digger laughed. "I'm reminded of that every day when I see your grumpy faces and hear all the dimwitted comments."

"Tell us again exactly what these are, Cap?" Harry held up the translucent items smaller than a postage stamp. He had a sheet of them in his hand.

Troy grabbed the sheet from Harry. The items arrived an hour before via the Paris station chief for the agency. "Digger, you're better at tech talk. Explain to the boys what these things are in their language. That means dumb it way the hell down for their sakes."

"Real funny, Cap." Sarge crossed his arms and frowned.

With a smile plastered across his face, Digger replied slowly, "They are really expensive and really fragile, so none of you morons should touch them, ever. You dig?"

Troy shook his head. "Try again, Einstein."

Digger got serious. "For several years, the Defense Department has tried to make some sort of tracking device for soldiers. The War on Terror got messy, and grabbing US soldiers became a top priority of the enemy. Our very own Cap knows about that all too well."

Troy shook his head in agreement. "Operation Scribe, that was a doozy." He paused for a second. "Ransoms are on the rise worldwide. These terrorist organizations, at least some of them, fund themselves through hostage-taking. Countries pay hefty ransoms, millions of dollars, in fact. Almost all of these instances are happening without the mainstream press acknowledging the entire scope of the global problem."

"But I read countries weren't paying ransoms." Jesús said.

Troy shook his head. "Total bullshit. It's all about optics. Just politicians posturing for their constituents. They are paying, and I'm talking billions of dollars per year globally!"

"So, back to these items." Digger held them up for everyone to get a good look. "Up till now, any attempt to actually put a GPS microchip in soldiers has been met with too much resistance by top military brass and also the White House. Technology limitations have also factored into that as well." Digger pointed to the translucent devices with his free hand. "They developed these marvels, which are tiny microchips that are sticky on one side. Basically, in the simplest terms, I can say they are global GPS tracking devices. They can be stuck on any surface, including human skin, and they are thinner than a piece of paper. Think of them as those press on tattoos we used to get when we were kids. These trackers are going to be placed on the inside bands of the money stacks being used to pay half the ransom."

"How many stacks are there?" asked Harry.

"Two hundred," replied Troy. "We have ten million euros on this table. One hundred bills per stack, each note worth five hundred, so that's fifty thousand per stack, times two hundred stacks you get ..."

"Ten million euros. We can count, Cap!" The Jackal exclaimed.

"In your head?" Troy needled. "And you didn't need a smartphone or Google? Impressive!"

The Jackal flipped him off.

"So how many sticky microchip GPS thingies do we have?" Harry asked in a slightly sarcastic tone. His IQ was about as high as Digger's. A dummy Doc was not.

"Twenty," Digger said. "We will spread them out across the two hundred stacks."

"Why'd we get only twenty?" the Jackal asked.

"Because of how much money a sheet of these little buggers cost," the colonel said as he came up behind the group.

"How much?" the Jackal asked. "Like the amount of my yearly salary?"

"Try salaries, plural," the colonel said.

"But won't they have some piece of equipment with them to check for tracking devices?" Jesús asked.

Troy nodded. "We are counting on them to have just that, and want them to scan that bag. They need to feel safe that the money is not being tracked somehow."

"Then we're toast," Jesús said.

"No, we would be toast if they worked like traditional trackers," Troy said.

"Say again?" Jesús looked at Cap with a puzzled look.

Troy looked at Digger. "Give them the simple version."

"Roger that Cap," Digger picked up a black device about the size of a cellphone. "Traditional GPS-enabled chips give off a signal, and you are correct. If you have the right equipment, like this device, you can do a sweep and pick up on the signal that is constantly emanating from them. These new microchips work differently. Simply put, they don't give off signals. At least not initially. The chips are programmed in advance to remain dormant for a pre-determined amount of time and only turn on to give off a brief transmission signal before they stop transmitting again."

"How long?" Sarge asked.

"These little buggers will be programmed to send a signal every hour after the drop time. The signal itself is a microburst. Less than a second."

"They will sweep the stack of money and find nothing that raises any alarms. And we can, in theory, track where they go with the money every hour?"

"That's right," Troy said. "We will have a location mark every hour where the currency is. Basically, a precise GPS coordinate at the time the transmission occurs from the twenty chips."

"And if they drop the two hundred stacks off in some bank vault in Paris?" the Jackal asked. "Or they split the money up?"

"Then we may be screwed," Troy said. "The signal itself can be tracked from anywhere on the planet, even inside a bank vault. But if they divvy up the money we'll have multiple locations to raid. If all goes to plan, they will bring the money back to their safe house. We'll know at that time how good Arjun's intel was and where the money is ..."

"Abby should be," Glenn said. He had been silent up to that point, and stood next to the colonel.

"Yes sir," Troy said. "At least that's our hope."

Glenn turned and looked to his right at the colonel. "I sure hope you and your men are on point about this plan."

"We are," the colonel said in the most reassuring voice he could muster. "We have reliable intel of the city they are holding Abby, but this should give us the actual address. Them asking for half the money upfront appears to have been a blessing in disguise."

Glenn nodded but appeared skeptical.

"Let's go over the plan one more time, fellas," Troy said. "We have two hours before we have to be at the tower, and I want to make sure everyone knows what I expect from them."

# 12

## PARIS FRANCE

### THE EIFFEL TOWER

Glenn sat at a round table in the far corner of Madame Brasserie, a contemporary Parisian restaurant located on the first level of the Eiffel Tower. He rubbed his hand along the white tablecloth and glanced to his left at the picturesque all-glass window, which provided a view of the Eiffel Tower's first-floor observation deck. From his vantage point, he could see every person who walked into the restaurant. Although there was no way for sure to know who would enter, his instincts told him it would be Nizar.

Three tables away, far enough to allow some space but close enough to get to Glenn quickly, Troy tried to blend in with the other restaurant patrons. His gaze focused on the restaurant entrance, then back toward Glenn. On the floor next to Troy, hidden from view, sat a large navy-blue duffel bag favored by many athletes. Inside it were two hundred stacks of currency which made up the ten million euros ransom.

Troy wore all black, a cross between a gangster and a hipster. A black dress shirt with ivory buttons and a black suit with no necktie. On the shirt, one of the ivory buttons concealed an embedded hi-def camera. Unseen by the naked eye, an earbud deep within his ear allowed him to hear the rest of his team. A microphone hidden under his collar allowed them to hear him.

Digger's voice sprang to life. "Cap, we have a person of interest who just entered the north lift. He matches Glenn's description of Nizar. He's on his way up."

Troy reached into his pocket and keyed the button to acknowledge he heard Digger. Using the pre-determined signal, Troy took his fork and banged it on the tabletop four times.

Glenn heard the repetitive thumps. His eyes strained even harder as he looked toward the entrance.

Two minutes later, Glenn watched as Nizar walked into the restaurant and approached the maître d'. After a brief exchange, the petite raven-haired woman motioned toward the rear of the restaurant.

As Nizar and the maître d' spoke, Glenn took his fork and rapped it hard on the table twice, which confirmed the target had arrived.

Troy keyed the button in his pocket four times in a row. The signal to the team meant *target acquired*.

The maître d' led Nizar to the far corner table. He looked around the restaurant as he followed the petite woman. She stopped at Glenn's table, Nizar thanked her, and he remained standing after she left.

Glenn looked up at Nizar, then at the empty seat across from him. His eyes seemed to say, *take a seat*.

"You're in my seat," Nizar said.

"Excuse me?"

"I require that seat, Glenn. I don't feel comfortable having my back to the entire restaurant."

"Of course, you don't." Glenn stood and moved to the opposite seat.

Nizar sat and looked around the table, a curious look on his face. "Where's my money?"

"It's my money," Glenn said. His voice did little to hide his anger.

"Not if you want your dear Abby back in one piece." Nizar's eyes scanned the area around the table once more. "So where is it?"

"I want proof of life first before I hand over the money."

"That is not what I instructed. Money first, then you will have your proof of life. Don't screw with me, Glenn!"

Glenn shook his head in a disapproving manner. "I want proof of life, or I walk. The money goes with me."

Nizar's face contorted, and a sneer formed at the corner of his cheeks. "Give me the money now, or Abby is dead, and you'll quickly join her in the afterlife." With those last words, he patted the inside of his suit coat. The motion implied he had a gun.

Clearly nervous, Glenn knew the next part of the plan would either be a success or a spectacular disaster. Failure would cause Abby's untimely death and maybe his own. He had to trust his friend Colonel Marshall and The Omega Group.

*God, they can't let me down.* He spoke the words as a silent prayer in his mind.

"Fine." Glenn snapped his fingers.

On cue, Troy removed the large duffel bag hidden under the tablecloth that dangled almost to the floor and approached Glenn's table.

Nizar saw the figure approach and reached for the gun under his suit coat jacket.

"Relax, you won't need that," the man in all black who stood before him said. "We have your money right here." He dropped the heavy bag on the tabletop between Nizar and Glenn with a loud thud. It made enough of a noise that people several tables looked over.

Nizar looked at the man in black, then back at Glenn. His hand still under his suit coat, the weapon not yet drawn out in the open, but his palm wrapped around the pistol grip tightly. "What have you done?" he hissed as he glared at Glenn. "I told you to come alone."

"You did," Glenn said. "And I don't trust you, Nizar. Not for one damn second."

"Trust? I trust you know that your actions here have cost Abby her life."

"Then we will leave with the money and be on our way if the deal is off," the man in black said as he reached out, gripped the bag, and raised it off the table.

"I'll take the money and still kill the girl," Nizar said.

The man in black pulled back his suit coat with his free hand to reveal a weapon of his own. "Like hell, you will. Ten million euros says I can draw faster than you and drill a bullet between your soulless eyes before you can even pull your weapon. All the while holding this bag of cash with my other hand." He shook the bag as he spoke. "Draw."

Nizar gazed at the brazen man intently, his hand gripped the weapon in the holster under his own coat tighter and tighter as each second passed. The man in black, his eyes disturbed Nizar. The look conveyed a stoic resolve rarely seen. This man had clearly killed before and would again. Nizar thought of himself as a tough man but didn't have a death wish. He was not a poker player and would not gamble now. He could see by the man's posture and build that he was serious about what he said. Nizar accurately guessed that he would lose to this man if he had to pull out his weapon.

"Care to try me?" The man in black asked with a confident tone.

His look caused a shudder to run through Nizar.

"The money is yours, Nizar. All we want is proof of life. You can have the money. Now, hold up your end of the bargain." Glenn tried his best to defuse the situation.

"You were supposed to come alone." Nizar's voice cracked and revealed a slight hint of fear.

Troy discerned the look in Nizar's eyes as he lowered the bag back onto the tabletop.

"Sit," Nizar said to the man in black as he gestured with his free hand and slowly removed his other hand from beneath his jacket.

The one word told Troy exactly what he needed to know. Nizar was a coward. He didn't have the balls to draw on him in the restaurant.

Troy grabbed a chair from the empty table next to Glenn's and spun it around so the backside faced the table. He sat down. "I'm here to protect Mr. Robert's interests and ensure his safety, nothing more, nothing less." He spoke the words to Nizar in a firm yet conciliatory tone.

Nizar's eyes darted from the man in black. and back to Glenn. "Open the bag. Let me see the contents."

Glenn unzipped the bag.

Nizar stood slightly, peered inside, then pulled out a few of the bound stacks of bills and brought them discreetly under the table. He used his thumb to flip through the stack. The money appeared legit.

"It's all there," Glenn said. "Count it."

Nizar shook his head. "That will not be necessary. If you shorted me, she'll be dead." He removed a device from his pocket and moved it over the outside of the bag. Placing the device inside the bag, he made several passes around the circumference of the interior. The device never made a sound. No tracking signals emanated from the bag.

Nizar said nothing, just grunted.

"Are we good?" Glenn asked.

Nizar didn't reply and instead pulled out his cell phone and dialed a number. He activated the speakerphone.

"Daddy." Abby spoke in a hushed tone.

Tears formed in Glenn's eyes. He had to fight hard to keep them from rolling down his face. Instead of answering, he glared at Nizar. "Put her on FaceTime. I want to see my little girl!"

"What?"

"You heard me. I want to see her, not just hear her voice. You agreed to show me physical proof, and just a voice is not good enough. I need to see her, know she is alive, and be sure this is not some audio recording of her calling out to me."

Nizar paused briefly, but after a few drawn-out seconds, he agreed. He hung up the phone and dialed a different number. "Put her on video," he said in Arabic. "Like we discussed."

Troy understood exactly what Nizar said. Arabic was one of the six fluent languages he spoke.

A few seconds later, Nizar handed the phone to Glenn.

Troy could see the screen as well, and the camera disguised as an ivory button recorded everything.

Glenn could see Abby. She appeared to be in a sparsely furnished, drab room with only a small cot and toilet in the background. She sat on a stool in the center of the room, heavy bars visible in the window behind her. Light shone through the bars and onto the floor next to her. Under the window, a small table, a metallic vase with a single flower, and a pink rose. Her left hand had thick white gauze bandages wrapped all over the spot where her severed finger would have been. The bandage was crimson red at the tip. Her clothes appeared soiled, and her hair was disheveled. Tears flowed down her face. Her right eye looked slightly bruised and puffy.

"Abby!" Glenn exclaimed. "Are you okay?"

"I'm alive, Daddy," Abby said. "Please do whatever they ask so I can get out of here."

"Have they hurt you?"

"Yes," she said. "But I am trying to be strong. I just want to be back home. Please get me out of here. I think I'm being held in—"

Before she could say another word, the video feed ended.

The screen on the phone went black.

"She's alive," Nizar said. "I have held up my end and showed you proof of life."

Glenn seethed as he looked at Nizar. "How could you do that to my baby?"

"I have shown you mercy today, Glenn, and will not the next time we meet. I could have killed her after you broke the arrangement and brought this hired dog as protection."

"Arf," the man in black said as a wicked grin spread over his face.

Nizar did not appear amused. "If you don't come alone for the second half of the ransom and I see this filth," he pointed directly at the man in black, "I will kill Abby without hesitation. Do I make myself clear?"

"Crystal," Glenn said.

Nizar rose from his seat and grabbed the duffel bag. Ten million euros felt heavier than he expected. "You owe me twelve million more," he said as he looked at Glenn. "An extra two million for bringing a hired gun which was not part of the arrangement."

"You'll get it. When do I get Abby back?"

"We will stick with the original date. I will contact you with the exchange location. Don't make the same mistake twice, Glenn, for Abby's sake." As he spoke, he brought his hand across his neck in a cutting motion. As he walked away, he said, "I'll be in touch."

Troy patted Glenn on the shoulder. "Let's get moving. It's time to go."

"Will the inducement work?"

"Time will tell," Troy said. "Hopefully, it allows us to get a fix on Abby's location."

## 13

## PARIS

Troy stayed with Glenn for protection. Even though Nizar departed with the cash, that didn't mean there wasn't someone else on the premises who might be a threat to Glenn. They had no way of knowing who made up the group that abducted Abby. After all, the initial cash drop might be a ruse to bring Glenn out into the open. The colonel instructed Troy to keep Glenn safe at any cost.

The other members of the team followed Nizar the moment he left the restaurant and descended to the base of the tower. With the oversized duffel bag slung over his right shoulder, Nizar stuck out amongst the throngs of tourists who scurried around the area under the tower like ants.

Two of the Omegas, Sarge and Jesús, followed directly behind at a safe distance, while the remaining three broke off the pursuit and made their way to a vehicle parked at Avenue de la Bourdonnais.

Still on the observation deck of the first level, Troy and Glenn watched as Nizar and the ten million euros moved farther away from the structure. The colonel stayed at the safe house and called the shots from afar.

Nizar walked at a brisk pace away from the tower. He headed northwest and moved as fast as one could when lugging around that amount of cash. Several times, he paused mid-stride and glanced behind. The gravel crackled under his footfalls, and he arrived a few minutes later at Quai Branly, where he climbed into an available taxi.

Sarge and Jesús closed the gap and slipped inside the next cab in the pullout. Sarge stuffed a wad of cash into the driver's hand and barked orders for the driver to follow the vehicle ahead of them. The French driver might not have spoken English, but he understood a thick handful of euros.

Both taxis maneuvered their way through the thick Parisian traffic as the car which contained Nizar headed east, away from the city center.

The entire team stayed in constant contact as Sarge relayed their real-time location as they followed Nizar's cab.

Thirty-nine minutes later, the taxi pulled up to the private terminal at Aerodrome de Lognes, a small airport east of central Paris. Nizar got out of the vehicle with the duffel bag clenched close to his body and he climbed aboard a private jet.

Sarge instructed the driver, in choppy French, to pull over a safe distance from the terminal. He and Jesús watched as Nizar boarded the plane.

Fifteen minutes away, Digger worked his digital magic from the back of a van. Based on the info relayed by Sarge, Digger hacked into the airport's systems.

"I've got the tail number," Digger said. "The plane was chartered by some LLC out of the Caribbean. I'm sure it will end up being some shell company. If Nizar and his team aren't complete hacks, they will likely cover their tracks pretty well."

"Keep searching," the colonel instructed over the comms.

"Roger that," came the reply.

Forty minutes later, the team gathered at the safe house outside of town and waited for the next GPS signals to display on Digger's laptop. The GPS locator gave the location of the aircraft in real time. The flight plan filed turned out to be false, which surprised none of them. Everyone stayed busy as Digger monitored the digital chatter. It took about six hours before they had enough data points, and the GPS signal stayed stationary for several pings. The time had come for them to pack the gear and move on.

"You are sure about the location?" the colonel asked as he hovered above Digger.

"Yes, sir," Digger pointed to the monitor in front of him. "The intel provided by Arjun proved accurate regarding the city they used. Since the signal has remained fixed the past few data transmissions, we have the specific coordinates where they brought the money."

"Great," the Jackal said with his typical sarcasm. "Not like that will be a tough place to operate."

"What do we do next?" Glenn asked.

The colonel got up from the chair he sat in and looked out the window. Nighttime arrived and his reflection showed in the panes of glass. "We have a compound in Crete. The team will stop there, get everything in place, then commence with the mission to get Abby back."

Troy had been silent for a while. He repeatedly watched the video of what happened on the first floor of the Eiffel Tower. Something about the video of Abby bothered him and not just how she had been treated. He analyzed the clip and pored over every detail.

The colonel noticed Troy's intensive glare as the video playback continued unabated. "What is it, Cap?"

Troy looked at him with a perplexed look on his face. "I'm not sure, Colonel."

"Is something wrong?"

"Maybe. I think so. I've got a hunch."

"Something you see on the video?"

"Uh, huh. But I can't quite figure out what it is yet."

"What do you want?"

"Some more time to watch it and think things over."

The colonel nodded in reply. "Let us know when whatever it is dawns on you. You've got the plane ride to figure out what doesn't feel right."

Troy frowned. "Copy that, sir."

"So, we land in Crete," Glenn said. "And then what?"

Troy, lost in his own thoughts, turned toward Glenn. "Then we change our tactics. It's time for us to stop playing defense and begin to play a little offense."

"Doing what?" Glenn asked.

"We're about to become the hunters!"

# PART IV - THE HUNTERS

# 14

## CRETE

### ISLAND IN GREECE

Waves lapped against the pink sand beach that led to an immaculate lawn dotted with palm trees expertly positioned around the property. A rectangular-shaped infinity pool with an oversized jacuzzi filled the space between the tree line and the three-level main house. Painted light yellow, the house reflected the sunlight, which made it hard to look at directly. The size of the compound made it resemble more of a resort.

Troy stood on the beach barefoot. The granules of sand filled the gaps between his toes. The warm sand felt delightful. A few steps away, the colonel wore brown sandals, which served as his idea of casual footwear. Troy had never seen the man barefoot in all the time they knew each other.

"The government owns this place?" Troy turned a full three-hundred sixty degrees as he surveyed the property.

"Umm." The colonel shook his head. "Not exactly."

Troy finished his examination of the property and settled his gaze on his commanding officer. "Spooks run it? I mean, this place has all the trappings of an agency complex."

"Not them either."

"Don't ask, right?" Troy delivered the question with a noticeable frown.

"Something like that," the colonel bit at the corner of his lip. "I'm always straight up with you, Troy, but all I can say is this place isn't owned by any entity tied to the US government. However, we have full use of the facilities anytime we need them and for however long."

"Which won't be more than a dozen hours or so," Troy said.

The colonel looked toward the sea and let out a sigh. "Correct, at least for this visit. Maybe our travels will bring us back here one day."

"Not your first visit here, I take it?"

The colonel just smiled.

Inside, Digger worked on the finishing touches of his equipment setup. Jesús, Sarge, and Harry helped him organize everything to turn the study into a makeshift command center. Several flat-panel monitors connected to his laptop showed various images of the target area. Satellite imagery was displayed on one monitor, while the other contained maps of the city. Information flowed across the screens nonstop. It would be a long night.

Fast asleep in a bedroom on the third floor, Glenn's constant snore sounded like a bear bellowing in the woods after an intense fight.

Exhaustion apparently took its toll on Glenn as he dozed on the flight from Paris to Crete. The colonel instructed his friend to rest as soon as they arrived. Glenn didn't argue, popped a few pills from a container in one of his bags, and headed straight for the bedroom.

Harry looked toward the stairs and then over to Jesús. "I was in boy scouts as a kid."

"I can see you doing that. We didn't have scouts where I lived in Los Angeles. They had gangs," Jesús said. "You preppy white kids made guns out of sticks while you were out in the woods. We had the real thing in east LA."

Harry laughed. "No doubt. Well, we had a great troop growing up. Troop 610 out of Western North Carolina. Our scoutmaster named Bud was a heavyset guy, but never judge a book by its cover. He could run like a gazelle if you got him into an open field. However, there's no question he was the loudest snorer I ever heard as a kid. Kept me up when we were out in Pisgah Forest or up at Camp Daniel Boone. But let me tell you, Bud's snoring didn't come close to the logs that Glenn is cutting up there."

Digger looked up from his laptop. "I built computers in my parents' basement when I was a teenager." He shrugged and looked back at the screen in front of him. "Geeks like me didn't get outside very often."

Harry looked over and shook his head. "I, for one, am shocked you didn't get laid until after basic training."

"My neighborhood in LA would have eaten both you pansies for breakfast," Jesús said.

Neither Harry nor Digger had a retort.

Outside, the Jackal roamed the perimeter solo. Given the choice, he preferred to do his own thing. Even though the colonel assured the Omegas the compound was secure, the Jackal insisted on checking things out himself. It gave him a chance to sneak outside and have a few smokes. The pack of Marlboro reds in his right front pocket wouldn't smoke themselves after all. Troy harassed him to quit since the day they first met, but so far, it didn't take. The Jackal marched to his own beat.

Back on the beach, Troy and the colonel continued their discussion.

"You watched that video dozens of times on the flight."

"I did," Troy said.

"What were you hoping to find?"

Troy paused before he spoke the next words. Finally, after an elongated moment, he posed a question. "You've known the Roberts family a long time, right?"

The colonel quickly replied, "Yes. Glenn and I attended West Point at the same time and roomed together when we were cows—"

Troy interrupted, "During your junior year?"

"Impressive!" The colonel exclaimed. "Most folks, even those in the army, aren't aware of the nicknames for the class structures unless they served as cadets."

"Plebes, yuks, cows, and firsties," Troy said with a smirk.

"You would have made one hell of a cadet, Troy."

"Not to be, sir, you know my story. Since I was a boy, all I dreamed of was joining the Bureau and following in Pop's footsteps."

"Life changes, huh?"

"In a heartbeat," Troy said. "All it takes is one hundred and fifty-eight grains to alter your destiny."

The colonel nodded and patted Troy on the shoulder. "You were telling me what bothered you about the FaceTime video."

Troy bit his bottom lip. "It's not one specific thing, but several minor details that aren't adding up, items that were out of place, things that didn't look right, at least in my mind."

"Care to indulge?"

"Not yet. Digger is working on enhancing the video for me. I want a clearer image of Abby and the room."

"Okay," the colonel said.

Troy looked down at the ground and pushed his feet deeper into the warm sand. "As soon as I have something concrete, I'll share it."

"Sounds fair."

"But I have a request."

"Name it."

"Abby's finger."

"What about it?" The colonel's eyebrows arched downward.

"Glenn said he left the box with the finger at his house in Houston."

"Yes, in the refrigerator so it wouldn't stink. What about it?"

"This request may seem odd."

"Troy, her severed finger is in a refrigerator. What could be more odd than that?"

"I want it tested."

"The finger?"

"Yes," Troy shook his head. "Her finger."

"Tested for what?"

"Not tested for something. I want a DNA test done on it."

The colonel rubbed his chin. "You mean to make sure it's hers?"

Troy nodded, "Correct."

"You really think it may not be Abby's finger?"

Troy shrugged. "I'm not sure what to think right now, but I'd like to ease my doubting Thomas mind."

"You're no doubting Thomas, Troy. Your faith is rock solid, and I believe in you. If you want the finger tested, we'll test it."

"What's the chance we can get that done ASAP?"

"Let me make a few calls. I have contacts who can help facilitate things stateside."

"Fair enough."

"In the meantime, head inside and see how Digger is doing with the intel gathered so far. We need a final plan agreed upon by the entire team in the next few hours. Time is not on our side. The deadline and last payment is less than forty-eight hours away, and we need Abby back before then."

"Copy that, sir."

The colonel smacked Troy on the upper back. "You and your men are going to get her back in one piece. I know it."

"Bet your ass we will, sir!" Troy turned and walked toward the main house. As he made his way around the pool, he spied the Jackal, who sat on one of the beach chairs.

The Jackal flicked his cigarette away as Troy approached.

"I've told you those things are going to kill you."

The Jackal responded with a smirk. "In our line of work, Cap, I'm more concerned about something that causes me a sudden stop instead of the drawn-out consequences of a long drag."

"They do say lead poisoning kills faster than nicotine."

"Yup, so I've heard, Cap."

# 15

## CRETE

The colonel stayed on the beach alone and waited until Troy was far enough away before he placed a call on the sat phone he removed from his back pocket.

Five thousand three hundred miles away, a person in a nondescript office building in Fairfax, Virginia, answered on the third ring. "What can I do for you, sir?"

"What type of assets do we have in the Houston area?" The colonel asked.

The line fell silent as the person looked at a file on his laptop. It took over a minute before the response arrived. A dull static sound filled the void. "Multiple types, but it depends. What do you need?"

"Access to a lab."

"What kind?"

"One that can process a DNA sample."

"Hold, please." The static sound returned for close to a minute. "Houston has several labs that should suffice. I can activate an asset there within minutes. Where's the sample?"

"A private home in West University Place."

A couple of seconds of silence passed as the person on the other end consulted their Google Maps. "There's a lab near the Galleria."

"Perfect." The colonel provided more specific details.

On the other end of the phone, the person made copious notes.

"Send your asset to the address I'm about to text you." The colonel took the phone away from his ear and texted the location.

"Got it," the person said.

"I'll need the test results returned in less than twelve hours. Can you arrange that?"

A sarcastic tone replaced the even keeled voice so far on the call. The person replied, "Well, sure, I'm a miracle worker, after all."

"Drop the attitude and make it happen," the colonel said in a terse tone. "This is important. Call me with the results as soon as you have them."

"Yes, sir," the person said.

"And keep this between us. No one else needs to know."

"Understood."

The line went dead.

Glenn's wife was not home. She flew to Santa Barbara with several of her friends the day before. The stress of the abduction made her decide to leave the house while Glenn traveled overseas. With nobody home, the asset could slip in, retrieve the finger, and get out. After the call ended, the colonel placed the phone back in his pocket and drew in a deep breath. The tropical breeze and distinct smell of the ocean breeze filled his lungs and slowed his elevated pulse.

<hr>

Three hours later, The Omega Group members, the colonel, and Glenn Roberts wrapped up an intense discussion in the make-shift command center. The conversation dragged on for over an hour, with the team members having many disagreements, which was not abnormal. It took a while to resolve the disputes and come to a consensus.

Glenn slept during the early part of the discussion and missed most of the arguments. He was only present for the final twenty minutes once they had hammered out most of the details.

The intel gained during Arjun's interrogation indicated the kidnappers held Abby in Douma, Syria, a suburb of Damascus. Numerous pings from the tracking devices placed on the ransom money confirmed the location. Since the tracking signal in the money bands didn't move for over eight hours, the team made the logical assumption: find the money, and we'll find Abby. However, without concrete proof, the Omegas argued for a while until everyone came on board with Troy's plan.

Unlike a typical military hierarchy, The Omega Group functioned differently. Even though the colonel ultimately made the final decision, and Troy led the men, each man's opinion counted, and one member's hesitancy mattered. If any of them felt they shouldn't move forward, they didn't. One voice could override a well-orchestrated plan. Of course, that was an extremely rare occurrence.

Syria proved to be one of the worst places for Abby to be held. Probably the only place worse in the region would have to be Iran. Yet, the team had no choice, and they would have to operate in the middle of an active war zone.

Not the first time and not the last.

The CIA maintained several deep cover assets in Damascus, and after several calls to senior agency staff, the colonel enlisted two men to be their eyes and ears on the ground to aid in their search for Abby.

# 16

## GREECE/SYRIA

The two agency assets slouched down as they sat in an old, silver-colored Mercedes 230E, their eyes barely visible over the dashboard. Both men chain-smoked, a hazard of the espionage job for many. Plumes of acrid smoke slowly leaked from the cracked windows. Jack and Bobby's names sounded American, but they were aliases. Syrian by birth, the same case officer recruited the two men while they attended the University of Damascus. Life within the clandestine organization started in their early twenties, with both men now pushing their mid-forties. A life lived amidst the chaos of a troubled nation proved to be all they knew.

Intelligence gathered from Arjun pointed to the city, but the tracker chips embedded in the money led to a quiet residential street in Douma, Syria. The stone house in question stood alone with empty lots on either side of the dwelling, unlike many homes in Douma, which sat right on top of each other. A seven-foot-high stone wall surrounded the home, another anomaly. On the other side of the wall, an arched wooden doorway was the only way inside the fortified structure. The distance from the walled entrance to the door of the house was around twenty paces. The center of the house contained a two-story open aired courtyard with a fountain in the center. A cherub atop a cloud adorned the center of the fountain with a constant stream of water shooting out of the cherub's mouth. Both the first and second floors contained four rooms each, a modest-sized home by Syrian standards.

Except for the occasional dog barking, silence engulfed the serene street. Several years earlier, the same street would have bustled with residents moving about most evenings. But not anymore, not with a civil war upon them. Syria changed dramatically as war encompassed the country. Few ventured out after nightfall unless they left their home heavily armed.

From the comfort and relative safety of the car, Jack and Bobby relayed real-time intel to The Omega Group.

In Crete, the call was on speakerphone.

"Do you have a thermal image?" Troy asked.

"Yes," Jack said.

"How many people are in the house?"

A moment of static. "Six."

"Where are they?"

"Four downstairs, two upstairs."

"Are all the windows in the house barred?"

Jack and Bobby talked amongst themselves for a moment. Jack answered. "Only the downstairs rooms. The upper-level windows have no bars, just shutters."

"Too bad the heat signatures couldn't tell us if any of them are girls," Sarge said.

"If only," Troy replied.

"Well, chicks run hotter, so maybe their color is darker on the thermal images." The Jackal stood back behind everyone else and had to get a word in.

"Moron." Troy shook his head. "Jack, what are the locations of the four people downstairs?"

"It looks like they are all in the center courtyard. Nobody is in any of the rooms."

"How about the two heat signatures upstairs?"

"In the same room. Top of the stairs to the left."

"I guess ..." Troy's words got cut short.

"We have movement," Jack interrupted. "Someone from the courtyard walked inside." Several seconds passed in silence. "Looks like one of them is on their way toward the front door."

Two minutes later, a man emerged. He walked on the opposite side of the road and past the silver Mercedes. The figure proceeded down the road. Bobby discretely took a picture of the man as he passed their car, and he quickly texted it to the team.

"A man left the house," Jack said. "I just texted his picture."

"Where's he headed?" Troy asked.

"Not sure. But there's a supermarket at the end of the road which is open late."

"I need Bobby to follow him. Let us know where he goes and what he buys."

"Understood."

Digger got the picture a minute later. Even though the image looked grainy, there was no mistaking the identity of the man.

The photo confirmed it was Nizar who exited the house.

Troy almost sounded giddy. "It's Nizar. We're in the right place."

"Understood. Bobby is following him now," Jack said.

A tense ten minutes elapsed in relative silence before Bobby got back to the car.

"Bobby is back," Jack replied.

"And?" Troy sat on the edge of his chair and tapped his foot on the ground.

"He made a grocery run," Bobby said.

"What did he buy?" Troy asked.

"Several grocery bags of food, two bottles of wine, and ..."

"And what?"

"Tampons, he bought a box of tampons."

"Good work, Bobby," Troy said. "You as well, Jack. We'll be in touch soon."

------◆◇◆------

The phone line disconnected, and Troy looked at the colonel, who nodded. No words between the two men were necessary.

Troy looked at the other members of the team. "Look, we got a lot of intel from Arjun indicating this is the correct town. The GPS chips prove that the cash is here, and we know Nizar is on site. The tampons are a stretch, but they give us an indication a woman is present."

"Or that the dudes inside are kinda on the freaky side," the Jackal said.

"Hey, I stuck one in my ear that time when I lost my earplug in that Mosul gun battle. That really intense one with the .50 cals. Don't you remember?" Sarge asked. "So, they certainly can serve more than one purpose."

The Jackal opened his mouth, but Troy cut him off with a hand gesture. "If you tell me some sordid story about the high school prom and a box of tampons, or what kind your mom uses, I'm going to shoot you in the dick. And enjoy doing so." Troy stared at the Jackal.

"Actually, the story involved a truck stop in upstate New York, two bottles of Titos, and a stripper I met at Scores in Manhattan." The

Jackal covered his crotch area with his hands as he spoke. "But damn, Cap. I'll shut the hell up now."

"That's a first," Troy said. "Someone make note of this momentous occasion."

"You think she's on site?" Sarge asked.

"We can't be certain, but I feel pretty damn sure we have Abby's location. Her kidnappers won't let her near any window or outside, and we have no way of getting any image from inside the house. I think she's there, even though I can't prove it." Troy looked around at the men who surrounded him. "Do you all agree?"

Everyone around the room nodded.

"Then there is only one thing left for us to do," the colonel said.

"Time for us to head to Syria," Troy replied.

# 17

36,000 FEET IN THE AIR

The team couldn't just fly into that part of Syria on account of it being an active war zone, so they needed another way into the country. That way turned out to be Lebanon, which borders Syria to the west.

The plan called for The Omega Group, including the colonel, to fly into Beirut, where a military helicopter would transport the team to the Beqaa Valley. The United States maintained friendly relations with the Lebanese military, and the colonel, after a few calls, got what he needed after handing out a few markers. From Lebanon, they would make their way across the Anti-Lebanon Mountains and into Syria. An arduous journey by truck, but the team couldn't risk flying over the mountains and arriving near Damascus via the air. It was common for helicopters to be shot at and destroyed. Syrian military or private aircraft, it made no difference. The Syrian Army and opposition forces targeted each other's aircraft unmercifully during the conflict.

The flight from Crete to Beirut took only two hours. Digger worked nonstop on his laptop the whole time. Besides confirming that the money remained in place, he continued to enhance the images Troy requested. Thirty minutes into the flight, he printed off a high-resolution image and handed it to Troy, who sat across the aisle from him.

"This is the best I could do, considering it came from the reflection on the metallic vase. I think it looks pretty damn good if I do say so myself."

Troy examined the photo and tried his best to memorize every detail of the man's face. "You did a great job, Digger. The facial features seem to match the man Arjun described."

"I agree," Digger said. "What do we do with the picture?"

"Get it over to Jack and Bobby. See if they can confirm they've seen him come in or out of the house."

"Will do."

Twenty minutes later, Digger got a call. He walked toward the front of the plane and interrupted Troy. "Sorry, Cap, but it's Jack. He said it's important."

"Put him on speakerphone." The colonel said. He sat across from Troy.

"I hear you sir," Jack said.

"You've got the photo?" The colonel asked.

"Yes sir," Jack said as the call cut out several times.

"Have you seen that man enter or leave the house?"

"No. And I'd be surprised if we did."

"Why is that?" Troy asked as the colonel grew silent.

"The man in this photo is well known within Syria," Jack said.

"He's a wanted terrorist, right? Ransoms? Sex trafficking?"

"Umm, no." Jack responded with an emphatic tone.

"Then who the hell is he?"

"He's the prime minister's son."

You could hear a pin drop in the plane's fuselage after Jack dropped the bombshell of all bombshells.

"You sure about that?" Troy asked.

"Without a doubt, he's a popular figure in Syria, and quite the ladies' man, according to the media reports."

"And has no ties to terrorism?"

"No, at least none that I'm aware of. He's just the son of a powerful politician."

Troy looked at the colonel, who stared right back and shrugged ever so slightly.

"What the hell is going on here?" Troy asked.

The colonel frowned. "The plot thickens, I guess."

"Maybe he's screwing Nizar." The Jackal raised his arms upward. "I mean, stranger things happen."

Troy rolled his eyes.

"Or maybe there's something else at work here." Sarge said as he joined the others at the front of the plane.

"What are you thinking, big guy?" Troy asked.

Troy trusted Sarge and his intuition.

"We may be new to this intelligence stuff, Cap, but we've both been around the block more than a few times. I think the old statement, *where there is smoke, there's fire,* may be at play."

Troy nodded in agreement. "I'm starting to think you're right."

# 18

## BEQAA VALLEY, LEBANON

The team arrived at a rustic farmhouse in the Beqaa Valley an hour after their plane landed in Lebanon. The remote airfield chosen by the colonel frequented by American intelligence and parties that wished to go unnoticed allowed them to enter the country with no oversight. With the gear unloaded, Troy went over last-minute intel as the team reviewed the plan they crafted on the flight from Crete. Everyone had a say in what would go down in Syria.

Digger worked his magic and confirmed the identity of the man in the picture, Farid Boutris. Jack's assessment of the prime minister's son proved correct no matter how much Digger searched. He could not reveal that the young man had any ties to terrorism or extremism.

Something didn't add up.

Also, the intel derived from Interpol confirmed Nizar's identity and left zero doubt about his connection to terrorism. He used his real first name with Glenn, not something expected. Foreign intelligence verified his full name was Nizar Faheem. He founded the terrorist group Ansar al-Mawt, and further digging revealed the group subsisted on kidnappings and ransoms throughout the region as its primary funding source.

For Troy, the pieces came together except for Farid's involvement. No matter how much they tried, Farid's role in the ransom made no logical sense.

Another thing bothered Troy. He sensed a change in Glenn after the live video feed. His expression and facial tics seemed different on the flight to Crete and also while they were at the safe house. Anger and fear were always present, but something new surfaced after Paris.

Guilt.

Most folks proved to be terrible at reading others, but not Troy. He had the natural ability to read people.

The colonel suggested they part ways with Glenn in Greece. No one on the team disagreed. They wanted as brief distractions as possible, and Glenn's emotions would likely prove to be a major hindrance.

Glenn did not protest or object when the colonel delivered the news. As the team left Crete, so did Glenn. He boarded his private jet, with a final destination of Israel, where he maintained a modest residence.

A knock at the door of the farmhouse broke up the lively conversation The Omega Group found themselves engaged in.

"Enter," the colonel said in his distinct voice.

The man hired to drive them into Syria stepped inside. "The truck is ready for you and your team, sir."

"Thank you," the colonel said. "We will be there in five minutes." After the driver closed the door and left, he turned back to his men.

"I'm still concerned about the extraction." Troy stared at his commanding officer.

"The same truck and driver that brings you in will be your transportation on the way out. You'll leave Douma and drive to Aana, a small town near the Lebanese border. There you'll rendezvous with a chopper; it will transport you back to Lebanon. I'll meet you, and we'll go together to Nazareth, where we will meet Glenn and reunite him with Abby."

"But if we are worried about anti-aircraft fire at the border on the way in, and that's why we are taking vehicles across the mountains, then how's it safe to take a helo on the way out?" Jesús asked.

"Good question," the colonel said. "A diversion is planned in a small town named Saghbine. It will attract any hostiles in that region and clear the skies near Aana as the chopper ferries you back across the Anti-Lebanon Mountains."

They talked for another minute before the colonel instructed the men to head out to the waiting truck and load their gear.

As the team made their way outside, the colonel grabbed Troy's shoulder to hold him back.

"You good, Cap?"

"Yes, sir," Troy said.

"Just bring her home safe, okay?" The colonel paused. "And at any cost."

Troy nodded. He knew what the colonel meant. "Will do, sir. Everybody will make it back. You have my word on that."

Troy joined the rest of the team in the truck.

As the team settled inside the vehicle, the colonel approached and leaned into the open window.

"I almost forgot one more thing. Dog tags. Hand them forward. None of you exist anymore, according to the Pentagon or the United States government. Active duty troops inside a Syrian civil war zone would be seen as an act of hostility. Plus, it would royally piss off the president. At the moment, he wants us nowhere near Syria under any circumstance."

"What a pussy," the Jackal said as he pulled his tags over his head and held them in his clutched fist.

"Soldier, that is your Commander-In-Chief," Troy barked as he held back grabbing for the tags and instead glared daggers at the Jackal.

"Sorry to bust your bubble, Cap. With all due respect, I'm being told to take off my dog tags, and my government will disavow me if I get caught. Or they'll let me get smoked and not even pay out my life insurance policy to my folks back home. Our aging Commander-In-Chief has never served a day in his whole life. Doesn't know what it's like to wear the uniform. Might not know what day of the week it is. Hell, he's never put his life on the line for his country. I think after all I've given to the military and my country I get to speak my mind, even call a spade a spade if I feel so inclined." The Jackal paused. "Sir." He glared back at Troy.

Troy let out a deep sigh. "God knows taking off dog tags has never stopped you from letting everyone know what you are thinking."

The colonel and the others remained quiet.

Nobody wanted to admit it, but the Jackal had a point.

"Damn, I hate this part," Harry said as he removed and passed his tags forward.

The Jackal gave his dog tags a kiss and added, "I'll see you babies soon, wait for me," before he placed them in Troy's hand.

"You're a sick man," Sarge said as he removed his own.

"A deeply troubled individual," Jesús said as he passed his tags forward.

"Hey now, Jesús!" The Jackal spun around in his seat. "You clutch your Bible. I clutch my dog tags. We'll see which one keeps us safe."

"You're screwed," Troy said as he stared at the Jackal. "In this life ... and the next!"

With a grin from ear to ear, the Jackal replied, "Ehh, probably, Cap."

"As long as you know it." Troy shook his head as he did a quick count of the tags and handed them off.

With the dog tags in hand, the colonel spoke. "Godspeed Omegas. Get your asses back safe and sound with Abby." He closed the door and moved away from the truck. "And if someone has to not make it back, be sure it's the Jackal." The colonel smiled and winked at the Jackal as he said the last phrase.

"Love you too, boss," the Jackal said as he blew a kiss.

The colonel smiled. "Just kidding. I even want the Jackal back. But if his vocal cords mysteriously get damaged, I won't lose any sleep over it." He stepped back and smacked the side of the vehicle hard with the hand that held the pile of dog tags.

The driver stepped on the accelerator, sending a cloud of dust behind the vehicle as the team began the arduous journey into Syria.

In the back seat, the Jackal hummed a familiar tune about how there was no rest for the wicked. Before long, the rest of the team joined in the melody.

A boy band, they were not.

# 19

## Douma, Syria

Three hours later, the team arrived without incident in Douma. Besides three security checkpoints, which they passed without question thanks to generous bribes, the trip across the border turned out to be uncomfortable yet uneventful. They met with Jack and Bobby a block away from the house and made a few minor tweaks to their plan after getting eyes on the target.

It was three a.m. (GMT+3) local time in Syria. The optimum time to hit the location when they expected the occupants of the house would be fast asleep. The last thermal scan confirmed no movements inside. Upstairs, two people were in the room farthest from the stairs.

Downstairs, one person was near the front door. The heat signature showed the person reclined but not moving. The other three heat signatures came from the back right room. They appeared to be lying in horizontal positions.

Everyone in the house appeared to be sound asleep.

On Troy's command, the men scaled the perimeter wall and took a position to breach the house through the front door.

Jesús placed the linear det-cord charge on the door. The recessed solid cedar door was a foot in from the stone walls of the house. Troy, Sarge, and the Jackal stood to the left of the door. Jesús, Digger, and

Harry to the right. The six men pressed tight against the exterior wall and waited for the concussive blast that would follow as the door blew to pieces.

Jesús held the detonator and waited for Troy to give him the signal.

Suddenly, Digger held up his arm with his fist.

*Hold tight.*

Digger removed the sat phone from his vest pocket and raised it to his ear. He listened and, in a whisper, said, "Yes, sir."

Digger motioned to Troy a few seconds later. "It's the colonel."

"Now?" Troy said in a hushed tone, irritated by the interruption.

"Yes." Digger handed Troy the sat phone. "Says it's urgent."

"What is it, sir?" Troy asked quietly as he pressed the phone against his ear. "We are about to blow the outer door."

The next few words confirmed his darkest suspicion.

"The finger," the colonel said. "DNA tests are back and conclusive. It's NOT Abby's ..."

Troy shook his head. "Shit. I hate being right."

# PART V – THE REVELATION

# 20

## DOUMA

Nizar slept soundly most nights, at least until the past few years. Middle age and BPH, or benign prostatic hyperplasia, robbed him of the joy that is uninterrupted sleep. Some days, it wasn't uncommon for him to wake up two or three times a night to take a piss. The commercials on the American satellite television he watched claimed frequent urination may be a sign of prostate problems, and one should get things checked out by a licensed physician. Nizar scoffed at going to a doctor and letting a man in the white coat examine his manhood.

"*Dammit,*" he said as he lumbered out of bed for the third time that night at three a.m. local time. Nizar shuffled over to the bathroom on the first floor, only to remember the toilet stopped flushing during his last visit.

*One of these fools must have clogged it once again.*

Begrudgingly, he made his way to the front of the house and the stairs that led to the second floor.

Nizar found Halil slumped in the beige-colored upholstered chair closest to the front door, sound asleep. An AK-47 lay on the ground next to him while his right arm dangled down toward the floor. Halil snored, and drool formed at the corner of his mouth.

*Some guard he is,* muttered Nizar as he walked past Halil and paused before he climbed the stairs to the only functioning toilet. Part of him wanted to kick the leg of the chair and watch as Halil crashed to the ground and woke up in a heap. But Nizar knew the endless bitching wouldn't be worth the temporary joy he would feel. Or would it? He pushed the devious thoughts aside.

He ascended the stairs slowly as his tired body ached, wanting nothing more than to climb back into the warm bed.

Two minutes later, as Nizar finished, he shook off the last drop into the toilet. Before he zippered the fly on his pants, a blast rattled the wooden floor. The explosion was close, too close. It startled him and woke him from his walking slumber.

*Did a bomb go off in front of the house?*

Nizar grabbed the bathroom door and twisted it with his left hand. At the same moment, he reached for his right hip and the holster, which held his .45 caliber Glock 21. It might be the middle of the night, but he didn't go anywhere unarmed, even for a late-night bathroom break.

With his mind swirling and pulse racing, Nizar pushed the door open and stepped into the hallway.

# 21

— ◆ —

# Douma

"Your call, Cap," the colonel said over the sat phone. "Abort or continue?"

Troy didn't need to think about it. His gut told him something might be off, but the only way to find out might be on the other side of the thick front door.

*Screw it.*

"We're going in, sir! I'll contact you after we have her." Troy ended the call and tossed the phone back to Digger.

"Blow the damn door, Jesús!" Troy exclaimed. "On my mark."

Time slowed for the Omegas right before the door frame splintered into a dozen pieces, and the remnants of the cedar door collapsed inward.

Troy gave the signal.

Jesús nodded and pushed the button.

In an instant, the ground shook, and the house quaked as the distinct popping sound of the explosives crackled as they pierced the silence of the night. The cedar door was a victim of the man-made material devised for maximum destruction.

On queue and before the fragments of the door even hit the ground, the men entered the structure. Their pre-assigned teams of three consisted of Troy, Sarge, and the Jackal responsible for clearing the second floor, while Jesús, Digger, and Harry were tasked with the main level.

The Jackal rushed through the door first, before it hit the ground, the barrel of his rifle leading the way as his keen eye searched for targets. Sarge followed on his six, with Troy right behind them both.

Armed for a mini war, the team carried HK416 assault rifles, a marvel of technological advances. The version they used included noise suppressors and laser sights. When fired indoors, the suppressed rounds sounded like a heavy book falling on a tabletop, not quite the unnoticeable whoosh sound Hollywood depicts with silencers, but not eardrum bursting either. The Jackal added an AG-C/EGLM 40 mm grenade launcher to his HK attached under the barrel and forward of the magazine.

As the Jackal entered the wide hallway, the stairs were located to his right. At the base of those stairs, a tango lay on the ground. The force of the det-cord and its concussive blast clearly knocked the sentry from his perch.

With the figure sprawled out on the floor dazed, the Jackal approached. Without warning, the tango on the ground stretched his arm out for an AK-47. As the tango reached for the Russian-made weapon that lay amongst splintered wood shards and debris, Troy and Sarge both saw the hostile movements. Neither one hesitated as Troy drilled a three-round burst into the man's chest while Sarge added two shots to the head.

"Tango one, down," Sarge said.

The Jackal swept the hallway as Troy took the lead and bounded up the stairs one at a time with both men behind him. Their feet moved swiftly yet made little noise.

Troy ascended the stairs, and halfway up, his earpiece came alive.

Jack's voice came through on the comms. "Be advised. Thermal images now show a third tango upstairs. Someone must have moved before the breach occurred."

"Roger that." Troy acknowledged Jack's intel as he angled his HK toward the top of the stairs. As he reached the last step, a figure emerged down the hall.

***

Nizar moved cautiously as he stepped out of the bathroom. The explosion followed by the suppressed gunfire rounds which came from downstairs made his pulse race dangerously high. He made a mistake and exposed himself as he stepped out into the hallway with his weapon drawn but not ready to fire. It turned out to be a fatal lapse in judgment.

A figure approached from the top of the stairs, and even in the dim light of the hallway, Nizar recognized the eyes before anything else. The piercing blue eyes seared into his mind. They belonged to the same man who was with Glenn in Paris at the Eiffel Tower.

The man dressed in all black.

Very few people intimidated Nizar, but the man in black elicited a fear within that few others could replicate. Nizar hastily raised his weapon to shoot, but knew the effort was fruitless.

In the end, the man in black bested him.

His last conscious thought ...

A four lettered vulgarity.

***

Troy recognized Nizar the moment they locked eyes in the darkened hallway. The red beam of Troy's laser scope placed a quarter-sized dot on his target. As Nizar raised his weapon, Troy didn't hesitate. With the red dot on Nizar's chest, Troy switched the firing selector from a three-round bust to a single shot. Next, he pulled the trigger twice. The first two rounds found their mark and tore apart Nizar's heart. As the body slumped to the ground, he delivered a third round, the insurance shot, between his enemy's eyes.

"Tango two, down," Troy said.

Troy, Sarge, and the Jackal kept moving. They stepped over the body and cleared the three other upstairs rooms before they approached the room where the two heat signatures previously showed, according to Jack and Bobby.

"Are there still two heat signatures in the far room on the second floor?" Troy asked Jack on comms.

"Affirmative," came the immediate response. "But they are moving."

Sarge approached and tried the handle, but the door wouldn't budge. Troy noticed the reinforced door was unlike the others in the house, and it contained a dead bolt-style lock.

Troy looked at Sarge. "Disable the lock, Sarge."

Sarge nodded and already had his Benelli M4 combat 12-gauge shotgun off his back, where he carried it in a sling and in the ready-to-fire position. He directed the barrel of the weapon to the locking mechanism and fired the breaching round, which destroyed the deadbolt with a single shot. He turned fast and, with his right foot, kicked the door as hard as possible. The force of his kick jarred the thick door open.

At that moment, sounds of automatic gunfire emanated from downstairs.

With all the explosions and rounds being fired, it would alert the neighbors to the operation, with local authorities likely dispatched within minutes, if not sooner.

*We need to move faster,* Troy said internally.

As soon as Sarge breached the door, Troy took point and moved into the room cautiously. Unaware of what he might find, his HK led the way as he searched for the two people believed to be upstairs.

*One of them better be Abby.*

# 22

## DOUMA

Jesús hurried past the body sprawled on the floor next to the stairs; he led Digger and Harry as they proceeded down the main hallway deeper into the house. After clearing the room to the left, the three men reached the kitchen, which they found empty. Dirty dishes covered the counter and filled the sink, the smell worse than the sight. Whoever stayed at the house did not abide by the saying *Cleanliness is next to godliness.*

A loud sound came from the adjacent room, a dull *thud*. Thermal images according to Jack showed the space contained two people only seconds earlier. The Omegas didn't know if they were both hostiles or possibly Abby and a guard. Because of the unknown, they could not rush in with HKs blazing on account of her unknown whereabouts.

Jesús, Digger, and Harry exited the kitchen and approached the room with extreme caution.

As they got close, Jesús, in the lead position, noticed the barrel of a gun protruding from the doorframe. "Hit the deck," he screamed a moment before the automatic gunfire sprayed across the wall at chest level.

Classic spray and pray.

*Amateurs.*

The three men dropped to the ground and lay flat. Chunks of wall fragments rained down on both men as they hugged the ground as round after round punctured the area above their positions. Digger, his weapon up first, toggled the selector switch to automatic fire on his HK and unloaded half a magazine toward the barrel and whoever pointed it in their direction. His consecutive rounds caused the barrel to withdraw from sight.

"Hit them and stagger the detonations," Jesús said as he pulled the flash bang from its pouch. If Abby was the second person in the room the explosion would startle her, but not do any serious harm.

A few seconds later, all three canisters tumbled into the room in rapid succession.

The three muffled explosions and blinding flashes of light disoriented whoever was in the room. Jesús, Digger, and Harry rushed inside and fired rapid bursts at two tangos who held weapons at the ready. The two hostiles within the room died in a hail of rounds before they could return fire.

"Tangos three and four down," Jesús said quickly as he tried to catch his breath. "No, Abby."

"Copy that," Troy said on the comms. "Continue your search."

Jesús, Digger, and Harry continued to sweep for any additional threats and doubled back to the front door.

"No other heat signatures downstairs besides you three," Jack confirmed on comms.

Once they searched the entire floor, Digger said, "Downstairs is clear."

"Copy," Troy responded. "You know what to do next."

Digger smacked Harry on the upper arm. "Okay, Doc, time to switch gears. Let's find that ransom money."

# 23

## DOUMA

The bedroom upstairs turned out to be larger than expected. With a brief glance, Troy surmised the dimensions to be about fifteen by twenty feet. The door opened near the corner of the room with much of the open space to the left. He quickly stepped inside, his weapon scanning in search of a target.

Since he and his team eliminated four tangos, Troy knew the last two people inside the house must be Abby and one of her abductors.

Troy detected two figures cornered at the far side of the room opposite his entry point. The taller figure hidden behind the smaller, slenderer figure.

*Abby.*

"Stop! Don't come any closer," the male voice called out from behind the smaller outline. "Or I'll kill her!"

Troy took four paces into the room and moved toward his left, then paused. Sarge followed his movements and paused at Troy's left side while the Jackal positioned himself to his right.

All three men had their weapons trained on the head of the taller figure.

Troy recognized Farid Boutris from the intel they reviewed before they breached the house.

Abby appeared okay. Except for the large caliber weapon pointed at her temple. Troy looked at her hands, all ten fingers visible. The index finger on her left hand, where she always wore Glenn's ring, looked intact.

"Are you okay, Abby?" Troy yelled across the room.

"Go away!" she screamed. "Leave us alone!"

Her response surprised Troy. *Stockholm Syndrome?* He wondered.

"She will die if you bastards don't leave now." Farid spoke forcefully, but the inflection in his voice conveyed a jumble of fear, aggression, and concern.

The three HKs painted beads on Farid's forehead. The red beams of light cut through the dimly lit room and gave off an eerie glow.

"Calm down, Farid," Troy said as his finger gripped the trigger and applied pressure.

A genuine look of surprise showed on Farid's facial features as Troy said his name.

Troy read his expression. "Yes, we know who you are and the title your father holds. You don't have to die here tonight. Just let Abby go. She's why we're here." He looked for a reaction but received none. Troy added, "You can keep the money and be on your way ten million euros richer."

"You think I'm doing this for money?" Farid's question came out with a hiss. The emotions spewed out from deep within.

"Do it, Farid, like you promised you would. Don't listen to him. Pull the trigger." Abby pleaded. "Now!"

As Troy looked at the two young people, he noticed two very different expressions on their faces. With Abby, he observed a resolve. *This girl truly wants to die*, Troy thought. Her eyes revealed her desire. Farid's expressions showed fear, panic, but also anger. This young man wasn't a trained killer and didn't want to pull the trigger.

But would he?

Troy couldn't take the chance. Even cowards build up enough resolve when pushed hard enough. All this flowed through Troy's brain in mere seconds.

"Do it, you coward," Abby said. "You promised me they wouldn't take me alive." She paused before she added, "Don't let me down like HE always did!"

The last phrase strengthened Farid's resolve, and Troy watched it take hold. He saw the straightened finger, which was completely off the trigger, curve and move to the firing position.

*Shit*, Troy thought.

Time for Troy to improvise. Shooting Farid with pressure on the trigger might cause his body to stiffen and result in Abby being killed. Troy raised his left hand. "Stand down, men!"

Farid's attention centered on Troy, and his command made Farid slacken the pressure on the trigger. He fell for the verbal ruse just as Troy hoped he would.

Troy moved his head slightly to the right and down. He gave the subtle signal only an operator would recognize.

As Farid straightened out his finger from the trigger, the Jackal saw his window of opportunity. With two rapid trigger pulls, Farid's head exploded in an destructive fury as bone, brain fragments, and gobs of blood blew out of the back of his head. His grip on Abby slackened, and his lifeless body crumpled to the floor. The gun he held did not discharge.

Troy believed it was over.

He was wrong.

# 24

## DOUMA

Farid's body hit the floor as the three soldiers approached Abby while lowering their weapons.

Her reaction shocked all three Omegas.

Abby reached down and picked up the handgun from Farid's limp grip and, in one motion, swung the gun upward.

Troy watched her movement. His weapon matched her motion, but it was clear Abby wasn't aiming for Troy or his men.

She planned to take her own life.

In a pure reactionary move, and knowing he only had one shot, Troy fired just as the gun Abby held reached the level of her shoulder with the barrel already pointing towards her head.

The bullet found its mark and struck the side of her right index finger while the round ricocheted off the trigger guard of the weapon, making a metallic clang sound as it did. Next, the round carried on and passed to the wall; it lodged inside the masonry.

An improbable shot.

For some.

Troy exhaled as the bullet buried deep into the wall.

Abby dropped the gun as her finger shattered. She screeched in agonizing pain as the three made it to her side.

"Secure her, Sarge," Troy commanded.

"Copy that, Cap." Sarge wrapped his enormous arms around her and, in one motion, had her up off the floor.

"Package is secure," the Jackal said into his comms.

A few seconds later, he received a response from Harry. "Ransom money located. It's all here."

"Evac now. Meet us at the front door," Troy said. "We're on our way down."

As they moved, Troy nudged the Jackal. "Grab Farid."

"What?" the Jackal asked.

"We can't leave the prime minister's son here. It will cause unwanted attention and may endanger the interests of the United States."

"You want me to carry his corpse? Half his fuckin' head is blown off! Are you serious?"

"I don't care," Troy said. "Drag him out of here by his pant leg for all I care. Just bring the body with us. That's an order."

The Jackal sighed. "Yes, Cap."

As they met up with the others near what remained of the front door, Troy looked at Jesús, Harry and Digger who had the duffel bag of cash slung over his right shoulder.

"Where'd you find it?"

"The bloodhound here found it," Digger said as he swung his head toward Jesús.

"Who me?" Jesús asked with a smile. "It's not my fault I got a nose for greenbacks."

"It was in the back bedroom closet. The floor was hollow, so we ripped up the boards and found the bag," Digger said as he patted the bag.

"What can I say, Cap?" Jesús shrugged. "All those years living that other life gave me a nose for cold hard cash."

"Well, good job finding it so fast. Now grab the accelerants, and let's torch this place."

Abby kicked at Sarge and tried to scream out. Troy had enough, and he reached for a tan neck gaiter he kept in one of his pant pockets.

"You should have let me die in there. Don't bring me to him!" Abby screamed with one last gasp.

Troy gagged her as fast as he could while Harry tended to her mangled, bleeding finger.

"Get her to the truck, Sarge," Troy said.

Harry finished bandaging the wound and nodded to Sarge. The field dressing was rudimentary but under the circumstances, it would do and at least temper the bleeding.

"You got it, Cap," Sarge said as he carried Abby out the front door.

Troy got the sat phone from Digger and called the colonel. "We have her, sir, starting the evac now."

"Good," the colonel replied.

"There may be an unforeseen issue," Troy said.

"What?"

"I'll tell you at the safe house."

"Can you handle whatever the problem might be?"

"It's not a whatever. It's a whoever, sir. I'll tell you face to face soon enough, and we'll work out a solution."

# 25

## DOUMA

Within three minutes, the team prepared the house and loaded every-one inside the truck. In the distance, sirens pierced the stillness of the night. The approaching sounds were not close but appeared to be getting louder. Troy started the incendiary device, and the flames engulfed the house as the vehicle headed away from the structure.

"An old piece of shit truck for our escape vehicle. Really?" the Jackal asked. "Couldn't the colonel have sprung for a cool ride like the Airwolf chopper to pick us up in the street in front of the house?"

"Stringfellow Hawke was busy," Sarge said.

The truck was an old military vehicle, and the team rode in the back under a canvas top. Jack and Bobby drove the lead vehicle to help at the various checkpoints along the way.

Everyone has a price, and Jack and Bobby knew how much each checkpoint guard required to stay silent and allow the team to reach the rendezvous location without incident. The two men would stay on point until they reached the border town of Aana.

As the truck bounced its way down the uneven roads, Troy reached out and thanked each man for their efforts and courage.

Troy paused as he got to the Jackal. "Good shot in there. Thanks for not hesitating."

The Jackal gave Cap a fist bump. "I got your six, brother. Always."

"I know you do, and I yours," Troy replied.

As the vehicle made its way along the winding roads, Abby tried to speak, but the gag made it impossible. It didn't stop her from fighting against the restraints they put on her. She also sobbed off and on at the pain that pulsated from her damaged index finger. Harry took off the field dressing and cleaned the wound after they left the house. His efforts were only a temporary fix, but they would ensure the wound stayed clean and avoided any infection.

Abby continued to protest in muffled tones, which got her little to no sympathy from the men tasked with bringing her back safely.

After a while, Sarge had enough. "Doesn't sound like the princess here wanted to be rescued." He glared at Abby as he spoke.

"No, you're right," Troy said as he and the others watched Abby continue to protest behind the gag.

Troy leaned in close and looked right into Abby's eyes. They burned with desire. One that told him she didn't want to go with him. "Don't want to go back to your father?" He had to yell on account of the noise from the old truck.

Abby nodded.

"That's ironic since it was your father who sent us to rescue you." Troy had enough and finally removed the gag from her mouth.

She coughed and gagged as phlegm shot out of her mouth and onto the floor of the truck. Saliva and clear liquid ran from her nose and mouth. She looked pathetic. "I have no clue what you know about my dad, but he's not a good guy. This whole thing is not what it appears," Abby yelled over the whine of the engine.

"Enlighten me," Troy said.

Abby looked around at all the men inside the truck who gazed at her. She saw no friendly faces. Then she looked down at the floorboard. Farid's cold, lifeless eyes looked up at her. She froze when she saw him like that.

"Fine," Troy said as she got quiet. "Have it your way. When we get back to Lebanon, you and I will have a little heart-to-heart chat. I doubt it will be pleasant for either of us."

She didn't look up at him and continued to stare at the corpse.

Troy glanced at Harry. "Give her something to help with the pain and let her sleep for a few hours, Doc."

Before Abby could protest, Harry had stuck a needle in her arm. A few seconds later, she slumped against Sarge and drifted off to sleep.

Besides Troy's words of encouragement and Abby's muffled yells, the team remained relatively quiet the entire ride.

"Dude," the Jackal said as he bumped Troy's shoulder.

"What?" Troy asked.

"You shot her, Cap."

"Yeah. So what? She was about to shoot herself."

"It's not that you shot her. I'm cool with that. It's where you shot her."

Troy looked back, puzzled.

"The index finger, it was the same appendage given to Glenn as part of the ransom," the Jackal said.

"Life is ironic in that way, isn't it? Maybe the universe has a sense of humor after all."

"Or she's a raving psychopath." The Jackal said.

Troy raised his eyebrows as he focused on the Jackal. "You really think the universe is a woman?"

"I mean, if it was a man, would it really be so chaotic? Look at the wacky weather we have. And hello? You ever heard of Mother Nature?"

Troy rolled his eyes. "You're so stupid."

# 26

## LEBANON

Abby awoke from her nightmare, only to find it far from over. Her eyes struggled to open and adjust to the light from above as a dull throb pulsated from her damaged finger all the way up her arm. She found herself in a sparse room. Fully upright, she sat in a wooden chair that creaked and groaned every time she shifted her weight. There was a folding table before her, and across from the table sat the man who rescued her in Douma.

"Good morning, sleepyhead," Troy said in a sarcastic tone.

"Is he here?"

Troy didn't expect this to be the first question she uttered as soon as she awoke. He analyzed her facial expressions. "Your father?" he asked.

"Yes."

"No, it's just us." Troy studied her face and watched as her features seemed to relax.

"Where's the colonel?"

Troy played dumb. "Who?"

"Colonel Marshall. He's the person my father must have called to rescue me."

"It's just you and me talking, Abby."

"And who are you?"

"My name is Troy."

"Did my father hire you and the others who stormed the house?"

"You could say that."

Abby looked around the room. Her eyes shifted back and forth like a dog before her gaze finally settled back on Troy. "You have nice eyes," she said.

Troy frowned. "Flattery won't work with me and will only hasten a one-way trip to Nazareth, where your father is right now. He expects us to bring you there. So, you better tell me why I shouldn't return you to him, and you better do it really damn fast."

"Whatever," she replied as she rolled her eyes. "You won't believe what I have to say, anyway."

Her attitude irked him, but he tried to remind himself of how old she was. "Here's how it's gonna work. I'll ask you a lot of questions. You'll answer them honestly because I'm like a human lie detector, Abby. If I think for a second you're not telling me the whole truth, I'll pull your little ass out of that chair and bring you straight to your father." He let his words resonate for a moment. "If you don't want to see him as much as I think, you'd be smart to be forthright from the get-go. Got it?"

Abby looked at the man across from her and focused on his eyes. A gateway to one's soul, she could see a steely resolve and had no intention of being handed over to her father. She knew she had no choice but to be honest. Several awkward seconds passed, and she said nothing.

"Do we have a deal?" Troy asked.

Abby nodded. "Deal. I want the truth out there. Not his lies."

"Then the truth may set you free."

Abby perked up at that comment.

Troy considered the order of his questions for a moment. Where to start was obvious. "You don't want to go back to your dad. That part is clear. So, let's start with a simple question. Why?"

"That's not as simple as you might think."

"Try me."

"My dad has a dark side."

"Lots of people have dark sides, Abby. It's called human nature. We're flawed creatures, after all."

Abby looked away before she slowly turned back. The undeniable look of shame washed over her face as she spoke. "I agree, but my father has more flaws than most average, loving dads."

Troy deduced where this was going. The hair on the back of his neck bristled. "He's been abusive to you?"

Abby nodded and, after she cleared her throat twice, replied, "Yes."

A lump formed in Troy's throat before he muttered. "Sexually?"

"I ..." Abby paused and never finished her statement.

Abby's silence spoke volumes and gave him the answer he'd prefer not to have. Troy felt his muscles tighten as a surge of adrenaline ran through his veins. Like pistons firing at full throttle. If there was one heinous act he hated more than anything else, it was the sexual exploitation of children. He had a zero-tolerance policy when it came to that unforgivable sin. Troy tried his best to engage in physical violence as a last resort, that is, until it had to do with child molesters. He'd gladly kill every fucking one with his bare hands if society didn't frown upon such acts of unprovoked violence.

A quiver ran through his body as he took a deep breath. He needed to think clearly before he pressed forward. For over a minute, an awkward silence lingered. "For how long?"

She sobbed. "Long enough, but one time is more than any daughter should ever have to endure."

Troy didn't need to ask any more about that. "How about physical abuse," he paused as his brain searched for the right words, "that was not sexual?"

"Yes, he abused me physically. I experienced years of emotional abuse as well. Although those scars are harder to show. The arm he broke in two places when I was fifteen still has a plate and two screws, so I can prove that one. The other instances were sporadic but at times still left scars."

"Why'd he break your arm?"

"I talked with a boy, and he didn't like it. We argued about it. Then he got physical."

"And it got explained away as what?"

"Lacrosse injury," Abby said.

"Your mother know about any of it?"

"My mom was more concerned about afternoon drinks with her girlfriends, and fitting in with the upper crust of society than to pay attention to what my dad did to me."

"How about your older siblings? Did he abuse them?"

She shrugged. "I have no clue. It's not something you bring up over Thanksgiving dinner. Right?"

"I guess not."

"Besides, they are so much older than me. I hardly talk to any of them. None of them moved back home after college. They only saw me as a spoiled brat after Dad made his riches, and I grew up with the extravagant lifestyle they all desired. I think they resent me. If Dad abused any of them, I would probably be the last person to know."

Troy nodded. "Just wondered if it was a pattern and you were just his latest victim."

"I have my suspicions but can only tell you what he did to me."

"How about the emotional abuse?"

Abby shook her head. "My father is a master manipulator. Most sociopaths are." Abby paused. "Besides, he's not the honest business-man everyone thinks he is. I saw things."

"What kind of stuff did you see?"

"Documents I wasn't supposed to read. Overheard phone calls I wasn't supposed to hear. My father projected a side he wanted every-one to believe. Then he had another side. The real him. Everyone has secrets, my dad has darkness."

"What kind of things was he into? Illegal business dealings?" Troy's eyes narrowed.

"More than just that."

"I'm here for the truth."

Abby let out a nervous laugh. "I hope you have a psychiatry degree, Troy, because I can tell you some doozies. How long do you have?"

"Look, I just want to get to the bottom of this, Abby."

"Okay, Troy, you say you want the truth? Want to know how deep the cuts go? Here goes ..."

⸻ ❖ ⸻

Forty-five minutes later, Abby finished her horrific tale. Troy wanted to believe she was lying but sensed what she said was the God's hon-est truth. Her sincerity dripped off each word that came out of her mouth.

Glenn was either a monster, or Abby must be the most compulsive liar he ever met. According to her story, his sins went much deeper than just what he did to his own daughter.

Troy believed Abby. He shook his head. "There's no easy way to switch gears after what you just shared, Abby. Thank you for your brutal honestly, but we need to talk about what just happened at the house. Tell me how Farid got involved. My team killed the prime minister of Syria's son and buried him in the mountains, so I'd like to know why. What was your connection to him?"

# 27

## Lebanon

Abby could not hide the exhaustion she carried within. As she continued to tell Troy about the ongoing abuse and her journey for freedom, the weariness showed on her face like a deep sorrow after an inconsolable loss.

Troy watched as Abby struggled and searched for the right words. A few times, he told her to take a break, but she pushed forward.

Abby continued. "Since you have my full bio, you know I took off this last year between high school and college."

"Yes, we know," Troy said, "but there are a lot of gaps in what we were told."

"Well, I needed a reason to get away from home since his abuse was growing worse. My goal was to avoid him at all costs, and he only allowed me to travel abroad because my mother insisted. I think she just wanted the house to finally be empty after thirty plus years of kids, but either way I milked it for all I could. But his leash would only be so long. A job with a nonprofit group presented itself. The organization has clinics around the Middle East which helps women displaced by the civil wars and sectarian violence that plague the region. Some folks might think I'm an entitled, selfish brat, but I care for people, especially women in need. So, on a trip to Damascus about three months ago, I met Farid at a club while out dancing one night. He took an immediate liking to me. One thing led to another, and well, he fell hard for me. It was the first time in my life that a man liked me for who I was instead of how much money my father had. Also, unlike my father, Farid didn't try to control me. I told him about my father, everything about him, and within a few weeks, we discussed how I could get away for good."

"Whose idea was the ransom? Farid's?"

"No, mine."

"But why a ransom?"

"It's simple," Abby said. "I needed money and wanted to start a new life. It seemed perfect. Ransoms are common in this part of the world, and they very often get paid. I researched them online."

Troy rolled his eyes. *Another Google expert.*

Abby continued, "I figured with the money, it would be easy to disappear, and he would never find me."

"Obviously not a well-thought-out plan," Troy said as he shook his head.

"Ya, I realized that before long."

"Farid was the son of the prime minister, so didn't he have money?"

"I didn't want his family's wealth, or even my father's for that matter. What I wanted was my freedom. I intended to use the money from the ransom to disappear forever, even give back and help the organization I was working with. If I used Farid's money, it would only enslave me to another man, something not acceptable. Ultimately, I felt it was my only way out of my life."

A manila folder sat on the table next to Troy. He removed a picture from the folder and slid it across the table in front of Abby. "Ever seen this guy?"

Abby looked at the photo. Her eyes narrowed. "Yes, once."

"Do you know his name?"

"No, he met with Nizar. It was the day things changed, and I realized my well-intentioned plan may have backfired."

"His name is Arjun Shakir. Basically, he is the finance guy for Ansar al-Mawt, a terrorist organization."

"I had no clue who he was, just saw him that one time."

"He provided us valuable intel, which allowed us to rescue you."

"And where is he now?"

"Gone. Down a black hole, never to be seen again. He will no longer aid terrorist organizations."

"Well, that's good," Abby said.

"How did Nizar and his men come into the picture? Our intel stated Farid had no ties to terrorism. Nizar is a different story. He's a known terrorist who kidnaps people for ransom."

"We tried to plan the ransom on our own, just Farid and I, but it didn't take long before it became clear we didn't know what we were doing. Farid reached out to Nizar through a connection with his dad. I never asked how they knew each other, if that will be your next question. Within a few days, after we met with Nizar, he made lots of suggestions regarding the ransom."

"And I take it things spun out of control when he got involved?"

Abby nodded. "Big time. I never asked for twenty million euros. I was going to ask for a few million. I'm actually not greedy. I just wanted a way to escape my situation. But Nizar acted insane and recognized an opportunity to make money, lots of money. He locked Farid and me in that second-floor room and flew to meet my father in Houston."

"Speaking of his meeting with your dad in Texas. What about the finger he gave your dad? Did you know about it?"

"Yes. That was all Nizar's doing."

"Where did the finger come from?"

"A local girl who died. She matched my body shape and hand size. They found her in the morgue, a victim of the ongoing war."

"It turned out to be a smart move on Nizar's part and a good way to get what he wanted from your dad."

"Nizar wanted to cut off my actual finger, but Farid convinced him to not harm me."

"Why did he split the ransom amount in half? Why not just get the money in one lump sum?"

"I never knew why," Abby said. "Maybe Nizar believed my dad wouldn't pay up, or at least not all of it. Like I said, as soon as Nizar got involved, we got cut out of the planning, and my dreams of getting money to start a new life vanished. I overheard a few things from the second floor where they held us, but not much."

"Where did Farid get the gun he had when we burst into the room? Nizar wouldn't have given him one if both of you were hostages."

"The day of the Paris meeting at the Eiffel Tower, when I saw my dad on camera. Nizar had his men bring us downstairs for the fake prison cell video. He set it all up before he flew to Paris. Farid created a distraction at one point and grabbed a gun after the video call ended. He stuffed the handgun away inside his waistband without anyone seeing what he did. Nizar's men turned out to be sloppy, and Farid hid the gun in our room. I remember seeing you in the background next to my dad, dressed in all black. Nizar ranted about the *man in black* the day he returned with the money. I think he was scared of you."

"What was Farid going to do with the gun?"

"We weren't sure what to do. I wanted to kill Nizar when he checked on us, but Farid figured we wouldn't be able to kill all of them with just the one gun."

"I doubt you would have either," Troy replied.

"We made a pledge to die together. No matter what happens. If Nizar tried to take me and give me over to my father, Farid promised to kill me. Then he would turn the gun on himself."

"A murder-suicide, huh?"

"Yes," Abby said.

"Did you love him?"

Abby considered the question for a moment. "I cared for Farid, and I am filled with a deep grief knowing he died because of me. But no, I didn't love him. I enjoyed his company. He was a generous lover, but after what my dad did, I'm not sure love is an emotion I can experience anymore in this life. Whatever life I'll have going forward."

"You still have your full life ahead of you, Abby. The future is not written. And love is not always something you try and find. Sometimes it finds you when you least suspect."

"Who's the lucky lady?" Abby asked.

"Excuse me?"

Abby smiled. "You married, right, Troy?"

The question surprised him, but he answered the same way he expected Abby to answer, with the truth. "No."

"Girlfriend or significant other?"

"Not really."

"But there's someone special in your life, or at least there was. I can see it in your eyes, hear it in your voice."

A connection formed between the two of them as they talked. Troy sensed she could read him better than others. He felt vulnerable at that moment, which was not a common feeling for him. Troy had been asking Abby to share her deep, dark past, but she knew nothing about him. He had gained her trust, even if she didn't have much of a choice.

"Her name is Cate." For the next ten minutes, Troy shared a story few outside his brothers-in-arms had ever heard. A story about a girl, one that still had a grip on his heart. What he shared about Cate and his past helped solidify their connection. At that moment, Troy decided there was no way in hell Glenn would get his daughter back. Troy wouldn't allow it, not then, not ever.

"Ever lose anyone you cared about, Troy?"

"Yes, many people, including both of my parents."

"How did you get over that?"

"It's difficult, and I'm not sure you truly ever get over it," Troy said. "I take it one day at a time."

"I'll blame myself for Farid's death the rest of my life. It was all my fault. None of this would have happened if it wasn't for me."

"Considering how my father died. Trust me. I understand all about guilt. But take it from someone who has battled that demon for over a decade. Guilt can eat you up inside and destroy the goodness within. That is, if you allow it to do so."

Abby nodded. "I'm scared, Troy. When I woke up, I was angry at you for saving my life, but now I'm not. I'm grateful you and your team came and rescued me, but I'm frightened about where to go from here."

Troy considered her statement for a minute and then stood. "I'll be back in a few minutes. Just sit tight, Abby."

The colonel watched the entire conversation from the closed-circuit camera feed. Troy walked into the room where he sat. The discussion was brief, and they agreed on what needed to be done. He returned to the room a few minutes later with the navy blue duffel bag.

Troy dropped the heavy bag containing ten million euros on the table.

"There's your freedom Abby. Take it."

Abby knew half the ransom had changed hands in Paris, but she never saw the actual money. She stood, leaned over the bag, and unzipped it. The stacks of money caused her to get dizzy. After a minute passed, she glanced back at Troy.

He could see the uncertainty in her eyes.

"Is this for real? You're letting me go? And letting me keep all the money?"

"Yes. You're free," he said with a warm smile. "After what your dad put you through, this money will not make you whole, but it's a start. We need to have your finger tended to and bandaged. You may need surgery. I'm sorry I shot you, Abby, but I had no choice."

"No. Don't apologize. You and your men saved my life! I see that now."

"This money will allow you the freedom to rebuild and create a new life. Not everybody gets a second chance, Abby. Nor do many people get a duffel bag filled with cash to start over. You'll have more opportunities than most, but never going back home can be a tough existence for someone your age. We have contacts that can help give you pointers on how to blend in, where to stash the money, and how to start a new life."

"But where should I go?"

"Wherever you want."

"I have no clue. My father always made all those decisions for me in the past. I can't believe he even let me be overseas as long as he did."

"Go somewhere far away," Troy said. "Maybe a tropical island."

"That sounds nice," Abby replied. "An island may work. I watched *Survivor* ever since I was a little girl. There are so many south pacific islands I'd love to visit."

"Just one piece of advice."

"Yes?"

"The tribe has spoken. Stay away from men for a while. Your recent track record isn't so great," he said with a smirk.

Abby smiled just a little, but the smile disappeared as fast as it had arrived. "I'm broken, Troy, and not sure I'll ever be made whole again."

Troy felt for the young woman before him. She had a heavy burden to bear. He reached out and coupled her two hands with his own. "Can I tell you something, Abby? Person to person?"

"Sure," she said. "I'd like that."

"Life's struggles can crush a person. They will ultimately either define you or refine you." His eyes locked on hers, and she stared back at him. "Everybody, no matter who they are, has obstacles in their life. But I see in you a fighter. Someone who has faced adversity and can navigate to the other side stronger. Better days are ahead for you, Abby. I believe that. One day you'll be a shining beacon for others. Maybe you'll be an advocate for women who find themselves in an abusive relationship. Not dissimilar to what you've endured."

Tears flowed down Abby's face, one big drop after another. "Thank you for those kind words, Troy."

"You're welcome."

"Can I give you a hug? Is that allowed?"

Troy smiled. "Sure, but don't tell the rest of my guys. I have an image of being a hard ass to my men that I must uphold. Besides, they give me enough shit daily. I don't want to give them any more ammo to use against me later."

"My lips are sealed." Abby came around the table and embraced him. It was a long hug, a tender yet firm connection. In a short period of time their souls connected on a level few people experience. As she let him go, she wiped the tears away. "You're a good man, Troy. My hero."

He didn't like being called a hero, but for whatever reason, this time, it didn't bother him.

# 28

TWELVE HOURS LATER

The members of The Omega Group sat on a private jet in Tel Aviv and waited for the colonel to arrive after his meeting with Glenn. He gave them firm orders to stay put and not leave the plane. None of them enjoyed being holed up in a confined area, especially something similar to an oversized aluminum can. As usual, the back-and-forth banter and ball-busting never abated. Those types of interaction were engrained into every fiber of who they were. However, the mood also had a somber tone at times, a palpable feeling of discouragement swept through the fuselage after a while.

Even though the ultimate mission was a success since they rescued Abby, her mental state and unmistakable anguish weighed heavy on each of them. Yes, even on the Jackal, who, deep down, if you ignored the sarcastic surface, had the biggest heart of them all. Each man processed in his own way not only the mission but the story Abby shared about how she grew up and the torment she faced. Getting an up and close view of human depravity damages those in its path in little imperceptible ways. Some things, once seen or told, can never be erased from one's mind.

Abby's injured finger required minor surgery; the procedure was facilitated in Jerusalem at the Hadassah Medical Center. An hour later, she left Israel via a chartered jet. Colonel Marshall, who had contacts virtually everywhere, orchestrated the flight but told the pilots to tell no one of the destination, even he would not know. Abby had a few minutes with the team to say her goodbyes and express her gratitude once more. Then she was gone. Nobody knew where she would go or if they would ever speak to her again. It was better that way. Abby had the colonel's contact info if the need ever arose, and she needed The Omega Group's help once more. Plus, Troy provided his personal email and phone number and told her to reach out to him for whatever she needed.

For over three hours, the team waited on the plane for their commanding officer to return. They all got very antsy and, before long, got on each other's nerves.

Finally, the colonel boarded the jet. His face betrayed how it went with Glenn.

"Denied it all?" Troy asked before the colonel even got three steps toward the center aisle.

"Every accusation," the colonel said. "He had an excuse and counterpoint to everything I relayed about Abby's story."

"And?"

"He lied nonstop, and it was clear as day." The colonel paused. "It's funny, well no, it's actually not. You think you know someone for a large portion of your life. Then one day, you come to find out it was all a lie. That's a tough egg to swallow, gents."

Troy could not hide the rage he felt toward Glenn. "What did you tell him?"

"Told him I never wanted to see or hear from him again. Then I threatened him. Said if he tried to reach out to Abby and find her, there would be severe consequences for those actions."

"You should have said we would hunt him down and kill him like hyenas," the Jackal said.

The colonel nodded. "I should have. Instead, after I said the phrase 'severe consequences,' I grabbed a cane leaning in the corner of the room and snapped it like a toothpick over my leg."

"That sounds expressive enough," Troy said.

"I think, in no uncertain terms, he got the hint," the colonel said.

"The question is will he take your advice?" Troy shrugged as he asked.

"For his own sake, he better."

"If he doesn't ..." Sarge didn't finish the rest of the statement.

———— ◆○◆ ————

It turned out Glenn heeded the advice.

For about six months.

# 29

## SIX MONTHS & ONE WEEK LATER

"It's done, sir." Mr. Blue hung up the phone and turned around in his squeaky office chair to face his boss. "As instructed."

"Any witnesses?" Mr. Grey got up from his chair and walked over. He stopped next to the cherry-colored desk of his subordinate.

"Of course not. He was alone when it occurred."

"And the other things?"

"Handled," Mr. Blue said.

"The money?"

"Moved to our accounts. Untraceable. More than we expected. Turns out not only was he a bad man, his vices and illicit businesses generated an immense cash flow."

"How much?" Mr. Grey asked.

Mr. Blue spun around in his chair and pulled up a document from his secure server. He pointed to the screen. "That much."

"Damn."

"Yes, I thought the same."

"What about all the records we removed from his place and any physical evidence tying him back to his misdeeds?"

"The originals are all locked in our vault located on the island. Everything else was scrubbed online or incinerated if it was a physical copy. There's no digital trail left to follow. If down the line people dig around all they will find is dead ends and false flags." Mr. Blue paused. "You didn't hire me for my good looks. I'm an expert at making shit go away."

"Good," Mr. Grey said as he looked down at his watch. "Time to make the call."

Mr. Blue nodded and picked up his iPhone. The call proved to be fast and to the point.

Mr. Grey tapped with his index finger on the desk as Mr. Blue spoke. His fingernail created a distinct sound with each strike.

After the call ended, Mr. Grey asked, "Well?"

"He said good job, and we better get started on the next directive."

"A man of few words. All action."

"Sure as hell better not piss him off," Mr. Blue said.

"Damn straight." Mr. Grey turned and walked back to his own desk. A phrase ran through his mind.

*Back to work.*

# EPILOGUE

## Tacoma, Washington

Exhausted and sore, Troy climbed out of his Ford F150 pickup truck and approached the tan-colored apartment building, which served as his home infrequently. For Troy, it had been three full days with little to no sleep. He never slept well on planes and just got off a military transport to Joint Base Lewis-McChord forty minutes before he arrived home.

As he walked into his drab, minimally furnished apartment in Tacoma, all he wanted to do was lay down and sleep. For a week, if possible. Maybe longer if only …

The chirping sound of his cell phone ringing disturbed his sleep fantasy.

*Damn, dammidy, damn*, he muttered to the empty space.

As Troy picked up his cell phone from the counter and looked at the caller ID number, it said the word "Unknown Caller." Few people had the number, and he figured it would be best to answer it. However, someone's timing really sucked.

"Yup," he said in a frustrated tone.

"Troy?"

He immediately recognized the voice. "Abby?" A jolt of concern ran through his body like a stray current from an exposed wire.

"Is this a bad time?" she asked. "You said to call ..."

"No, sorry. It's just that ... well, I've been away for a while and returned stateside within the past hour. Are you okay? Where are you?"

"I'm okay, still abroad."

"What do you need? We haven't spoken since Jerusalem six months ago."

"I'm calling about the news."

He looked down at the phone. "What news?"

"You know," she said. "The news about my dad."

"What about him?" Troy noticed an uptick in his pulse. "Did he try to find you?"

"No." There was a pause on the line. "Ummm ... I thought you knew."

"Knew what?"

"He's dead, Troy."

"What!" Troy exclaimed. "How?"

"He died earlier today. The news station in Texas said it was a boating incident, an accidental drowning."

"Wow, Abby. I'm shocked. I'm sorry, but I don't know what to say."

"Really? You didn't know about it?"

"Absolutely not. This is the first I've heard."

"Well then, this is a little awkward."

"What?" Troy asked.

"I mean, I kind of called to say thanks."

"Thanks?" The words she said perplexed him. "For what?"

"For taking care of him. Well, at least I figured when I heard the news, it must have been you and your team that did it."

"My team? Why would you think that?"

"Well, for starters, you guys rescued me. And the colonel threatened my father if he tried to track me down. Plus, the news said he died at the lake."

"What's so odd about him dying in a lake? He owned a boat, right?"

"My dad hated the water, and not many people knew that. Yes, he had a nice big boat, but he only took clients out to schmooze them and close deals. He wouldn't have been out fishing by himself and drowned like the news said. And I thought your group went after him. You had just waited for enough time to pass as to not raise any suspicions. Then made it look like an accident."

"I can assure you it wasn't us. Our job duties are hard to explain, but we're not killers for hire. The taking of life is always a last resort for us."

"Oh," she replied.

"I'm not sure what to say, Abby. Maybe it was just as the news said, an unfortunate accident."

An awkward pause ensued. Abby let out a deep breath. "Yeah, well, I don't believe that, Troy."

Troy waited a moment before he replied. "If you would like I have someone I can call at the FBI."

"Yes, I know who Kate works for, Troy. You told me all about her job."

"No, I'm not talking about Kate. There is someone else. When I was deployed in Iraq, I met a guy named Eli Payne, he was part of the Third Ranger Battalion. We did a couple operations together. Eli is someone I trust. He's out of the military now and works for the FBI in the Washington DC field office. We speak from time to time. I could make a call and see if he could make some inquiries into the drowning. Eli will keep things on the down low."

"That's not necessary, Troy. But thanks for the offer."

Troy sensed the apprehension in her voice. "Abby, to be clear, my team has been overseas for the past three months and had little contact with the outside world. You can believe me when I tell you that your dad fell off our radar after we rescued you. We most certainly had nothing to do with your father dying."

"I'm sorry to have bothered you, Troy. And I didn't mean to infer you and your team were ruthless killers."

He could discern the remorse in her words. "That's okay, Abby. There's a lot you don't understand, and I'm sure it's a very difficult time for you. I'm glad you called and checked in. I've been worried about you. Are you good? I mean, you can't be good after news like this, but ..."

"Yes," she interrupted before he could finish. "I'm relieved he won't come for me. My father died a long time ago in my mind."

"I can understand why you feel that way. Someone you trust should never violate you in such a way."

"When Colonel Marshall confronted my dad in Nazareth," she paused. "Well, what did my father say?"

"Denied the whole thing. Said he never laid a finger on you, called you a spoiled brat, and a compulsive liar. Said he and your mom sent you away in the hope you would mature and get a better understanding of how well you actually had it. He claimed that if the ransom was just a big hoax, then it was because you wanted his money."

"My dad was full of shit."

"I know. We didn't believe anything he said."

"It meant a lot that you and your team believed me."

"Every word. I knew the moment our conversation began that you were being sincere. After interacting with your father, I also knew that there was something off about him."

"Thanks, Troy."

"You're welcome, Abby. Since he's dead, will you come back home for the funeral?"

"No. I'm not ready to face my family. Not yet. I don't blame them per se, but I'm also not ready to see them either, at least not for a while."

"Understandable. What have you been doing with yourself?"

"Well, for starters, I took your advice and explored several new cultures in far-off lands. It's a great big world out there. For the first few weeks, I found a small island nation in the South Pacific and simply rested. The island is only accessible twice a week from Air New Zealand. It became my special place. I've gone back several times. You'd probably really like it there."

Abby told him all about the island.

"I bet I would like it there. Maybe one day I'll find myself on those beaches," Troy said.

Abby continued. "Then I started more adventurous travels. And yes, to answer your next question, I've stayed away from guys. I've been very discreet and not been flashy about the money or where I stay. Been doing my best to avoid trouble, keep a low profile, and come to grips with who I am and what I want out of life."

"I'm glad to hear that," Troy said. "You deserve happiness, and you should never settle for less. Time will heal most of your wounds, Abby. Betrayal by a family member is by far one of the deepest cuts you can endure, but this too shall pass."

"What about you? Speaking about happiness, what did Cate say when you contacted her?"

Troy blushed, although Abby had no way of knowing it. He stammered in his response, which was out of character for him. The only other person to make him do that was Cate the first time they met. "I didn't reach out to her. N-n-not yet," he replied, slightly embarrassed.

"What? You told me you would when we last talked before I boarded the plane to leave Israel."

"That's true," he admitted. "And I will. I need the time to be right."

"That's a lame excuse. There's no time like the present, Troy. You told me that yourself."

"I hate when people use my advice against me," he replied with a groan.

"Hang up and call her."

"Maybe," Troy said.

Abby scoffed at his response. "Maybe? Are you serious right now? Man up, Troy! Call the girl."

It was a playful tone, and he could tell, but still gave her grief. "Did you tell me to man up? After I saved your ass in Syria?"

"True, but you also shot me. Not exactly a chivalrous thing to do."

"Good point," Troy said with a laugh. "But that was one hell of a shot."

"Yes, it was. And I'm glad you took it and spared me from myself during that dark time in my life. Thank you. Again."

"You're welcome, Abby."

"Look, take my advice for a change instead of giving it. Call Cate and tell her how you feel."

"You're right," Troy said. "I will. It's been way too long."

A few minutes later, the call ended. Troy was glad he answered the call. They had agreed to stay in better contact going forward. Abby held a special place in his heart. She had taught him valuable lessons in those brief moments their paths crossed. He never had a little sister, but if he had, Abby would be the one he'd choose.

As Troy glanced over at the counter, he looked at the framed picture of Cate. It was like she stared right back at him. She looked drop-dead gorgeous in that Boise State University sweatshirt, even better when it came off. It was his favorite picture of her.

God, he missed her.

Her mind.

Her body.

Her soul.

Troy looked at Cate's picture, then his phone, and finally back at the picture. A smile formed at the corner of his mouth as he scrolled through the contacts, and his finger hovered over the green call button.

The End

Troy Evans and The Omega Group will return ...

# Acknowledgments

Bringing the character of Troy Evans from initial thought to published work took many years. In fact, it took more years than I expected. But everything has a proper time and most of life does not go as we expect or plan. Age has taught me that some of life's greatest gifts come when we least expect them, and they sure as heck are difficult to achieve. Publishing has been no exception.

I dreamed up the Troy Evans character and started mapping out my first book in early 2014. By mid-year, I started my first novel, titled *Vengeance*, and completed it while at Yosemite National Park. Troy was the protagonist of that initial story, and the Omega Group first graced the pages at that time. Two more novels and several novellas later, I still did not get published. However, instead of getting discouraged, I pivoted and put those initial writings aside, crafted new characters and wrote a novel titled, *The Body Man*. Actually, the book title came before anything else, and I built the world around that singular concept – Who is *The Body Man*? Several years after I completed the first draft, TBM would become my debut novel, published in November 2021. The writing journey I took from 2014 to 2021 was a long and bumpy path. Smooth and short just wasn't in the cards, and honestly I'm okay with that. Most things that come easy in this life don't satisfy for long. It's the things we struggle with the most that provide us the greatest joy.

Troy's character always called out to me in the recesses of my mind as I wrote other things. I knew I had unfinished business until Troy came back to life (at least in my mind). The opportunity to share him with the world always nagged at me over the years. While waiting on my second novel to work its way through the publishing realm (which hit a few snags but will be out in 2024), I switched gears once more and put my energy back into Troy and *The Omega Group*. I felt renewed; it was like meeting up with an old friend and starting back at the same place you left off years earlier. *Ransomed Daughter* is the first in what I hope will be many stories to release (featuring the characters you just read). The guys can be a little rough around the edges. These men operate in a world where you question everything, even authority, and sometimes go with your gut even when the intel seems cut and dry. (Authors note: very few things in life are cut and dry). I hope you enjoy Troy's journey and share his adventures with others.

For those of you still struggling to finish your first manuscript, or maybe find an agent, especially those trying to get a publishing deal (or deciding whether to self-publish) I offer the same two words I tell myself regularly. No matter which path you choose. NEVER QUIT. Believe in yourself even when the world appears to be rooting against you. If you can muster the courage, persevere, and be your biggest advocate ... you can succeed. That's a FACT, not a statement.

My thanks go to ...

**I Am**. For all my blessings (which are many).

To my children, **Bruce** and **Noelle**. I believe in both of you. And love you, always.

**Mom (Patty)** is my biggest supporter.

**Dad (Thomas)** was the person who handed me my first thriller.

My brother and sister, **Brett** and **Jackie** as they both embark on new journeys in life.

Grateful to the rest of my **Family** (there are lots of you).

I've got some of the greatest groups of **Friends** a man can have. I'm blessed to go through life with each and every one of you. Whether it's local friends like the fathers from **Troop 610**, others far away who I rarely see, or even my annual **Pinehurst** golfing buddies; truly it's an honor. Here's to many more years and even more adventures.

**Max (The Pope) Council**, one of my oldest and closest friends. Thanks for always being there.

Blessed to have the friendship and support of **El Presidente - TC Thompson**. Grateful for the countless conversations around story ideas, marketing, family, and what we want to do when we grow up.

Stories focusing on *The Omega Group* and **Troy Evans** contain a few subtle head nods to my college roommate **Andrew Reinertsen**. He dropped out of school and fulfilled his lifelong dream to join the army. My flag collection from around the world is thanks to him. Stay safe while you are out there fighting the "polar bears."

The **Writing Community** and many **Scribes** I've met so far along this journey have been a source of encouragement and help. My sincere thanks to each of you.

My Beta readers: **Adam Hamdy, Jeff Clark, Drew Ward, Mark Elliott, John Guarnieri, Ama Adair, Max Council, Todd Wilkins, Steve Stratton, TC Thompson, (Dr. Dr.) Dave Richards**, and **Jack Stewart**. Thanks to each of you for your insight, encouragement, and honest feedback. This novella is better because of you. Any faults therein lie with me as the author. And yes, I'm sure there are a few errors.

Ransomed Daughter is my 2nd published work and I would be remiss if I did not mention all the podcasters who had me on their programs to help promote my debut novel, *The Body Man*, over the past two years. **John Guarnieri - Speartalk, Jason Piccolo - The Protectors, Jeff Clark - Course of Action, David Temple - The Thriller Zone, Fred Burton - Ontic, Glenn Pasch - You're In Charge, Claudia King - Strong Enough, John Stamp - That's Criminal, Reden Dionisio - Foris Et Fidelis,** and **Sam Whitfield - The Whitfield Report**. Also, thank you to **Noah George** of the **George Real Estate Group** for having me on my 1st radio interview on **WHKP Radio 1450/107.7**.

I put together my own mini book tour when *The Body Man* came out in late 2021. It's been a lifelong dream to meet readers and sign my books in person. See folks, dreams really do come true. Several people helped make this dream a reality. Thank you to **Jennifer & Madison McCray**, and of course **Brian Wohnig (The McWoh's)** for hosting the event held in Virginia. I also made my way down to Georgia and had a event at **Red Top Brewhouse** with the help of my cousins **Karen & Scott Machan**. Finally my local hometown Carolina event was held at **Open Road Coffee** thanks to **Stan Yoder**. Beyond humbled for everyone that came out to see me at those three events. Let's do it again for *Ransomed Daughter*!

Thank you to the team at **Best Thriller Books** for their support of my debut novel and also this one. **Stuart Ashenbrenner, Chris Miller, Todd Wilkins, Derek Luedtke, Steve Netter, Kashif Hussain, David Dobiasek, Ankit Dhirasaria,** and their fearless leader, **James Abt.**

A special note of thanks to **David Darling, Joe Goldberg, Jeff Clark**, and **Ama Adair** for their above-and-beyond help to me as I brought *Ransomed Daughter* to life. Their assistance was very much appreciated. This novella was new territory for me and these terrific

**Scribes** helped immensely as I brought it from concept to finished product.

Thank you to Author **Steve Stratton** for the many calls over the last few years and for listening to my rants about the publishing journey. Here's to new ventures.

I've called author **Adam Hamdy** my mentor, and he has kindly reminded me of the **Seinfeld** episode dealing with mentors. (Note: almost every part of life can be referenced back to that show somehow) Instead, I'll say he is my friend, a source of encouragement, and one heck of a writer. If you're not reading books written by Adam, you need to start now.

**Brad Meltzer**, by his actions and words has indirectly taught me how to treat others and above all how to lead the way. Keep blazing the trail.

A special thanks goes out to **John Guarnieri** of **Speartalk - Security Podcast** and COO for **Silver Spear Security**. John brought me on his podcast in 2022 to discuss *The Body Man*. Over the course of the year, we started a project together, and I attended 8 **Shinedown** shows. Those shows turned out to be incredible experiences that spanned coast to coast and even across the pond to the UK. Forever grateful for all the support John has showed *The Body Man* and now *Ransomed Daughter*. Bring on the Reaper.

Thank you to **Brent, Barry, Eric, Zack,** plus the entire (and incredible) crew who make up the band, **Shinedown**. Special thanks to **Hoogie** for starting my pick collection. The band and crew allowed me a peak behind the scenes, a view very few people get to experience. I'm extremely grateful for the opportunity. If you don't listen to **Shinedown**, you need to start. And if you've never been to a **Shinedown** concert you are truly missing out. Go, and go often.

Thanks to **Todd Wilkins** for the superb cover and digital creations. I can't recommend his services enough.

Go to **www.jtoddwilkinsphotography.com** to learn more.

Grateful to **Fernando Menotti (Nando)** for the graphic design assistance.

Edits were provided by **Jonas Saul**, Chief Editor at Imagine Press Inc. Thank you, Jonas.

Thank you to my friend **Kathy Lubin** & **Danita Sartin** for giving the manuscript one final pass.

I'm grateful for the opportunity to start **BruNoe Media Publishing**, and look forward to what will happen down the road.

Finally, to my **Audience**, thank you for giving me your most precious commodity, your time. It's something you never get back and I don't take the fact that you spent your time on my story for granted. I hope you enjoyed this novella. I always strive to learn and improve. Hope you'll stick with me for the long haul. As I've been saying for a few years now, I'm just getting started. Life's a journey, not a destination. Join me ...

Eric P. Bishop

July 2023

# BREACH OF TRUST (COMING IN 2024)

## A SNEAK PEEK

Chapter 1
West Wing
The White House

Sometimes dying is the greatest escape.

———— ◄O► ————

The Body Man sat down and let out a weary, elongated sigh. Some days lasted an eternity while others passed like a vapor. This day was the former versus the latter. He leaned back in the worn-out black leather office chair; the movement elicited a sharp squeak from the overused parts. Often, he slept in the chair, or on the couch across from the desk, more so than his own bed. The incident in the Gulf of Mexico changed everything for The Body Man, as his home no longer acted as a sanctuary. Danger lurked behind every corner, a knife raised in the air ready to strike, or at least that's what he feared as he stepped into each room. As the chair rocked with a slight tremor, he squeezed the bridge of his nose with his thumb and index finger; he gave enough pressure to elicit a wince.

A thick file, each page stamped *Classified* in bold red font, lay spread across the cherry desk. The pages a constant reminder of how close he came to not only losing his own life but crippling an entire nation.

The past only able to stay where it belonged when he could learn to let go and move on.

Yet, he could not.

With an office only a few doors down from the Oval, unequivocally the most revered office in the world, The Body Man occupied what most people would say was priceless real estate within the White House.

He extended his legs straight as the heels of his Italian shoes rested precariously on the desk's beveled edge. As exhaustion set in, his eyes involuntarily shut.

When they opened, he found himself in a different place. He was there, back on the oil platform in the middle of the Gulf.

Kidnapped, beaten, drugged, and tortured, the memories flooded back like blood through an artery.

*I'm dreaming.* He muttered.

The Body Man looked around the drab interrogation room, and recognized not only the space but also the smells that permeated his nostrils. Next, he glanced down at his garb, the outfit identical to what one would see adorning a prisoner. The orange jumpsuit hung loose on his muscular frame. His hands held in place with thick steel cuffs connected via chain to a large ring in the center of the stainless-steel table. Likewise, his feet restricted by shackles clasped around his ankles held firm by the mechanism connected to the floor.

Trapped with no way to escape, the feelings returned. He welcomed death, the embrace of what was to come.

No fear.

No regrets.

Only a deep resolve stirred deep within.

Minutes passed in silence until the sound of the interrogation room door opening caused The Body Man's gaze to shift away from his clenched hands and towards the ajar door. Shadows obscured the face of the man who entered, but The Body Man's eyes tracked him as the figure strode into the room and circled the steel table several times like a hunter sizing up its prey, gauging the best moment to strike.

A feeling of déjà vu wrapped itself around The Body Man like a weighted anxiety blanket covering a person consumed by fear.

The man stepped into the dim light that surrounded the table. He looked familiar, but The Body Man could not place where he knew the man from. He had thick dark hair and several days of stubble. The mysterious figure stared at him with a look drenched in contempt.

"My name is Peter Casha," the man said after several agonizing moments of silence.

*That name. I know that name.* Still something felt off.

Silence engulfed the room like a thick fog.

A minute passed. "Are you here to free me, Mr. Casha?" The Body Man asked.

"Yes, I guess you could say I'm here to set you free."

Again, déjà vu. The familiarity of the moment overwhelmed his senses.

He knew this moment. Like a distant memory just out of reach, buried deep within ones subconscious.

Without provocation, Casha lunged at The Body Man. While at the same moment he pulled a hidden blade from beneath his shirt. The hilt made of ivory; the blade crafted by a bladesmith with exquisite taste and skill.

In vain, The Body Man attempted to stand and remove a hidden, sharpened pencil. The object he filed down using the metal bedframe where he slept each night since he arrived. The makeshift shiv stuffed into his waistband, unseen by his abductors. A pencil verses a blade sounded like a ridiculous pun, but it's all he had to defend himself.

As he reached for his waistband, the action proved to be in vain as the man across from him, now halfway across the table, thrust the sharp blade into his chest repeatedly with quick, precise almost surgical motion, before he could pull out the pencil.

*This is not how it happened. It's all wrong.* The words ran through his mind like water sliding over a smooth rock.

A searing, unquenchable pain ravaged The Body Man as the force of the slices drove him back down into his seat. His cuffed hands reached to his chest as he tried in vain to apply pressure to the hemorrhaging wounds. Blood gurgled up from within like molten lava escaping its subterranean vault.

Several seconds later he pulled his trembling hands away, the appendages covered in dripping, crimson colored blood.

His hands moved to his forehead and gripped his brow as he looked down as the bloodstain on his shirt continued to grow larger by the moment. In his peripheral vision, he could make out the figure of the man move closer as he looked to raise the weapon once more.

"Oh, and by the way." Casha now towered over the slumping figure of The Body Man. "Greetings from President Steele. He wanted you to know. Death comes for us all."

A sudden and loud sound caused his drooped head to jerk violently as the thick office door swung open with enough force to strike the metal stopper mounted to the wall. His hands, a fraction of a second earlier, cuffed and drenched in blood, now clenched his wet forehead. Beads of sweat covered his brow, followed the contours of his face, and left a darkened mark on the collar of his shirt.

As he pulled his hands away from his head, his eyes focused on the sweat which covered his hands. No red, no blood. Only perspiration covered his skin.

"You still here, Nick?" The voice asked just over his right shoulder.

Nick Jordan, The Body Man, sat upright in the chair and shook his head slightly to get the cobwebs out.

The flashback, intertwined in a dream, with part fact and part fiction, recessed back into his subconscious as his apprentice brought his attention back to the present.

"Yeah, Sam. Still here." Nick scooped the contents of the file back into the folder and tucked it within the desk drawer, locking it before he put the keys back into his pants pocket.

Sam eyed Nick with an eyebrow arched upward. The thick beads of perspiration clearly visible on his head to his neck. "Are you ok?" A concerned tone articulated in Sam's voice. "You're soaked in sweat."

"All good, just dozed off. That's it."

Sam didn't appear to believe his fib. "Yeah, right. Still having the nightmares?"

"Who, me?" Nick shrugged. Expression of weakness not really his style.

"You can't live in the past, boss. At least not indefinitely. Nor can you run from it. This isn't the first time I've come across you like this, and I doubt it will be the last. Maybe you should go talk to someone.

And by talk with someone I mean, a professional. Not just lie to me each time I ask how you are.”

Nick nodded. “Copy that, I’m good, Sam. Seriously. Just trying to tie up a few loose ends. And besides, I don’t need a shrink. I got this.”

“Well, at least go home. Your bed misses you.”

“What’s a bed?” Nick asked, his tone dripped with sarcasm.

Sam pointed to the thick office door that led to the hallway of the West Wing. “Look, tough guy. It’s that way. Get the hell out of here, go home, and find out.”

# About the Author...

Eric P. Bishop grew up in Connecticut, and relocated to the South after college. Moves to the Rockies and the Pacific Northwest occurred before finally heading back East to raise a family.

After many years in corporate America, he turned his passion for the written word into reality and chased his dreams of crafting novels.

Eric lives in Western North Carolina with his children, where they explore the great outdoors most weekends while he dreams up his next adventure. See www.ericpbishop.com for more about Eric and his work.

# ENJOY THE JOURNEY ...